Contents

Contents

The Aleph
(1949)

PENGUIN BOOKS

The Aleph

'He more than anyone renovated the langauge of fiction and thus opened the way to a remarkable generation of Spanish-American novelists. Gabriel García Márquez, Carlos Fuentes, José Donoso, and Mario Vargas Llosa have all acknowledged a debt to him'
J. M. Coetzee, *New York Review of Books*

'Borges was the quintessential writer's writer . . . he proved himself to be one of the towering figures of literature in Spanish'
James Woodall, *Guardian*

'I love his work because every one of his pieces contains a model of the universe or an attribute of the universe . . . because his stories often take the outer form of some genre from popular literature, a form proved by long usage, which creates almost mythical structures' Italo Calvino

'What Borges offered his readers was a philosophy, an ethical system, a method . . . for the craft of following a revelatory thread through the labyrinth of the universe' Alberto Manguel, *Observer*

'He creates, outside time and space, imaginary and symbolic worlds. It is a sign of his importance that, in placing him, only strange and perfect works can be called to mind' André Maurois

'He is the seer who appears, as if in a dream, to lead the votary forward . . . In one essay he says of Joyce that "he is less a man of letters than a literature". We may without hesitation apply the same description to Borges himself, with the codicil that his is the literature of eternity'
Peter Ackroyd, *The Times*

JORGE LUIS BORGES

The Aleph
Including the Prose Fictions from *The Maker*

Translated with an Afterword by Andrew Hurley

PENGUIN BOOKS

PENGUIN BOOKS

Published by the Penguin Group
Penguin Books Ltd, 27 Wrights Lane, London w8 5tz, England
Penguin Putnam Inc., 375 Hudson Street, New York, New York 10014, USA
Penguin Books Australia Ltd, Ringwood, Victoria, Australia
Penguin Books Canada Ltd, 10 Alcorn Avenue, Toronto, Ontario, Canada m4v 3b2
Penguin Books India (P) Ltd, 11, Community Centre, Panchsheel Park, New Delhi – 110 017, India
Penguin Books (NZ) Ltd, Private Bag 102902, NSMC, Auckland, New Zealand
Penguin Books (South Africa) (Pty) Ltd, 5 Watkins Street, Denver Ext 4, Johannesburg 2094, South Africa

Penguin Books Ltd, Registered Offices: Harmondsworth, Middlesex, England

These translations first published in *Collected Fictions* in the USA by
Viking Penguin, a member of Penguin Putnam Inc. 1998
First published in Great Britain by Allen Lane The Penguin Press 1999
Published with a new Afterword in Penguin Books 2000
The Aleph, Including the Prose Fictions from 'The Maker' published as a
separate volume in Penguin Classics 2000
1

Copyright © Maria Kodama, 1998
Translation and notes copyright © Penguin Putnam Inc., 1998
Afterword copyright © Andrew Hurley, 2000
All rights reserved

This selection was originally published by Emecé Editores, Buenos Aires,
as the collection *El aleph*

The moral right of the translator has been asserted

Set in 11/13.25 pt PostScript Monotype Columbus
Typeset by Rowland Phototypesetting Ltd, Bury St Edmunds, Suffolk
Printed in England by Clays Ltd, St Ives plc

The Immortal ✳

In London, in early June of the year 1929, the rare book dealer
Joseph Cartaphilus, of Smyrna, offered the princess de Lucinge
the six quarto minor volumes (1715–1720) of Pope's *Iliad.* The
princess purchased them; when she took possession of them, she
exchanged a few words with the dealer. He was, she says, an
emaciated, grimy man with gray eyes and gray beard and singularly vague features. He expressed himself with untutored and
uncorrected fluency in several languages; within scant minutes he
shifted from French to English and from English to an enigmatic
cross between the Spanish of Salonika and the Portuguese of
Macao. In October, the princess heard from a passenger on the
Zeus that Cartaphilus had died at sea while returning to Smyrna,
and that he had been buried on the island of Ios. In the last
volume of the *Iliad* she found this manuscript.

It is written in an English that teems with Latinisms; this is a
verbatim transcription of the document.

I

As I recall, my travails began in a garden in hundred-gated Thebes, in the time of the emperor Diocletian. I had fought (with no glory) in the recent Egyptian wars and was tribune of a legion quartered in Berenice, on the banks of the Red Sea; there, fever and magic consumed many men who magnanimously coveted the steel blade. The Mauritanians were defeated; the lands once occupied by the rebel cities were dedicated *in æternitatem* to the Plutonian gods; Alexandria, subdued, in vain sought Cæsar's mercy; within the year the legions were to report their triumph, but I myself barely glimpsed the face of Mars. That privation grieved me, and was perhaps why I threw myself into the quest, through vagrant and terrible deserts, for the secret City of the Immortals.

My travails, I have said, began in a garden in Thebes. All that night I did not sleep, for there was a combat in my heart. I rose at last a little before dawn. My slaves were sleeping; the moon was the color of the infinite sand. A bloody rider was approaching from the east, weak with exhaustion. A few steps from me, he dismounted and in a faint, insatiable voice asked me, in Latin, the name of the river whose waters laved the city's walls. I told him it was the Egypt, fed by the rains. "*It is another river that I seek,*" he replied morosely, "*the secret river that purifies men of death.*" Dark blood was welling from his breast. He told me that the country of his birth was a mountain that lay beyond the Ganges; it was rumored on that mountain, he told me, that if one traveled westward, to the end of the world, one would come to the river whose waters give immortality. He added that on the far shore of that river lay the City of the Immortals, a city rich in bulwarks and amphitheaters and temples. He died before dawn, but I resolved to go in quest of that city and its river. When interrogated by the torturer, some of the Mauritanian prisoners confirmed the traveler's tale: One of them recalled the Elysian plain, far at the ends of the earth, where men's lives are everlasting; another, the peaks from which the Pactolus flows, upon which men live for a hundred years. In Rome, I spoke with philosophers who felt that to draw out the span of a man's life was to draw out the agony of his dying and multiply the number of his deaths. I am not certain whether I ever believed in the City of the Immortals; I think the task of finding it was enough for me. Flavius, the Getulian proconsul, entrusted two hundred soldiers to me for the venture; I also recruited a number of mercenaries who claimed they knew the roads, and who were the first to desert.

Subsequent events have so distorted the memory of our first days that now they are impossible to put straight. We set out from Arsinoë and entered the ardent desert. We crossed the lands of the Troglodytes, who devour serpents and lack all verbal commerce; the land of the Garamantas, whose women are held in common and whose food is lions; the land of the Augiles, who worship only Tartarus. We ranged the width and breadth of other deserts—deserts of black sand, where the traveler must usurp the hours of the night, for the fervency of the day is unbearable. From afar I made out the mountain which gives its name to the Ocean; on its slopes grows the euphorbia, an antidote to poisons, and on its peak live the Satyrs, a nation of wild and rustic men given to lasciviousness. That the bosom of those barbaric lands, where the Earth is the mother of monsters, might succor a famous city— such a thing seemed unthinkable to us all. Thus we continued with our march, for to have regressed would have been to dishonor ourselves. Some of the men, those who were most temerarious, slept with their faces exposed to the moon; soon they burned with fever. With the depraved water of the watering holes others drank up insanity and death. Then began the desertions; a short time afterward, the mutinies. In repressing them I did not hesitate to employ severity. In that I acted justly, but a centurion warned me that the mutineers (keen to avenge the crucifixion of one of their number) were weaving a plot for my death. I fled the camp with the few soldiers who were loyal to me; in the desert, among whirlwinds of sand and the vast night, we became separated. A Cretan arrow rent my flesh. For several days I wandered without finding water—or one huge day multiplied by the sun, thirst, and the fear of thirst. I left my path to the will of my horse. At dawn, the distance bristled with pyramids and towers. I dreamed, unbearably, of a small and orderly labyrinth at whose center lay a well; my hands could almost touch it, my eyes see it, but so bewildering and entangled were the turns that I knew I would die before I reached it.

II

When I disentangled myself at last from that nightmare, I found that my hands were bound behind my back and I was lying in an oblong stone niche no bigger than a common grave, scraped into the caustic slope of a mountain. The sides of the cavity were humid, and had been polished as much by time as by human hands. In my chest I felt a painful throbbing, and I burned with thirst. I raised my head and cried out weakly. At the foot of the mountain ran a noiseless, impure stream, clogged by sand and rubble; on the far bank, the patent City of the Immortals shone dazzlingly in the last (or first) rays of the sun. I could see fortifications, arches, frontispieces, and forums; the foundation of it all was a stone plateau. A hundred or more irregular niches like my own riddled the mountain and the valley. In the sand had been dug shallow holes; from those wretched holes, from the niches, emerged naked men with gray skin and neglected beards. I thought I recognized these men: they belonged to the bestial lineage of the Troglodytes, who infest the shorelines of the Persian Gulf and the grottoes of Ethiopia; I was surprised neither by the fact that they did not speak nor by seeing them devour serpents.

Urgent thirst lent me temerity. I estimated that I was some thirty paces from the sand; I closed my eyes and threw myself down the mountain, my hands bound behind my back. I plunged my bloodied face into the dark water and lapped at it like an animal. Before I lost myself in sleep and delirium once more, I inexplicably repeated a few words of Greek: *Those from Zeleia, wealthy Trojans, who drink the water of dark Aisepos . . .*

I cannot say how many days and nights passed over me. In pain, unable to return to the shelter of the caverns, naked on the unknown sand, I let the moon and the sun cast lots for my bleak fate. The Troglodytes, childlike in their barbarity, helped me neither survive nor die. In vain did I plead with them to kill me. One day, with the sharp edge of a flake of rock, I severed my bonds. The next, I stood up and was able to beg or steal—I, Marcus Flaminius Rufus, military tribune of one of the legions of Rome—my first abominated mouthful of serpent's flesh.

Out of avidity to see the Immortals, to touch that more than human City, I could hardly sleep. And as though the Troglodytes could divine my goal, they did not sleep, either. At first I presumed they were keeping a watch over me; later, I imagined that my uneasiness had communicated itself to them, as dogs can be infected in that way. For my departure from the barbarous village I chose the most public of times, sunset, when almost all the men emerged from their holes and crevices in the earth and gazed out unseeingly toward the west. I prayed aloud, less to plead for divine favor than to intimidate the tribe with articulate speech. I crossed the stream bed clogged with sandbars and turned my steps toward the City. Two or three men followed me confusedly; they were of short stature (like the others of that species), and inspired more revulsion than fear. I had to skirt a number of irregular pits that I took to be ancient quarries; misled by the City's enormous size, I had thought it was much nearer. Toward midnight, I set my foot upon the black shadow—bristling with idolatrous shapes upon the yellow sand—of the City's wall. My steps were halted by a kind of sacred horror. So abhorred by mankind are novelty and the desert that I was cheered to note that one of the Troglodytes had accompanied me to the last. I closed my eyes and waited, unsleeping, for the dawn.

I have said that the City was built on a stone plateau. That plateau, with its precipitous sides, was as difficult to scale as the walls. In vain did my weary feet walk round it; the black foundation revealed not the slightest irregularity, and the invariance of the walls proscribed even a single door. The force of the day drove me to seek refuge in a cavern; toward the rear there was a pit, and out of the pit, out of the gloom below, rose a ladder. I descended the ladder and made my way through a chaos of squalid galleries to a vast, indistinct circular chamber. Nine doors opened into that cellar-like place; eight led to a maze that returned, deceitfully, to the same chamber; the ninth led through another maze to a second circular chamber identical to the first. I am not certain how many chambers there were; my misery and anxiety multiplied them. The silence was hostile, and virtually perfect; aside from a subterranean wind whose cause I never discovered, within those deep webs of stone there was no sound; even the thin streams of iron-colored water that trickled through crevices in the stone were noiseless. Horribly, I grew used to that dubious world; it began to seem incredible that anything could exist save nine-doored cellars and long, forking subterranean corridors. I know not how long I wandered under the earth; I do know that from time to time, in a confused dream of home, I conflated the horrendous village of the barbarians and the city of my birth, among the clusters of grapes.

At the end of one corridor, a not unforeseen wall blocked my path—and a distant light fell upon me. I raised my dazzled eyes; above, vertiginously high above, I saw a circle of sky so blue it was almost purple. A series of metal rungs led up the wall. Weariness made my muscles slack, but I climbed that ladder, only pausing from time to time to sob clumsily with joy. Little by little

I began to discern friezes and the capitals of columns, triangular pediments and vaults, confused glories carved in granite and marble. Thus it was that I was led to ascend from the blind realm of black and intertwining labyrinths into the brilliant City.

I emerged into a kind of small plaza—a courtyard might better describe it. It was surrounded by a single building, of irregular angles and varying heights. It was to this heterogeneous building that the many cupolas and columns belonged. More than any other feature of that incredible monument, I was arrested by the great antiquity of its construction. I felt that it had existed before humankind, before the world itself. Its patent antiquity (though somehow terrible to the eyes) seemed to accord with the labor of immortal artificers. Cautiously at first, with indifference as time went on, desperately toward the end, I wandered the staircases and inlaid floors of that labyrinthine palace. (I discovered afterward that the width and height of the treads on the staircases were not constant; it was this that explained the extraordinary weariness I felt.) *This palace is the work of the gods*, was my first thought. I explored the uninhabited spaces, and I corrected myself: *The gods that built this place have died.* Then I reflected upon its peculiarities, and told myself: *The gods that built this place were mad.* I said this, I know, in a tone of incomprehensible reproof that verged upon remorse—with more intellectual horror than sensory fear. The impression of great antiquity was joined by others: the impression of endlessness, the sensation of oppressiveness and horror, the sensation of complex irrationality. I had made my way through a dark maze, but it was the bright City of the Immortals that terrified and repelled me. A maze is a house built purposely to confuse men; its architecture, prodigal in symmetries, is made to serve that purpose. In the palace that I imperfectly explored, the architecture had *no* purpose. There were corridors that led nowhere, unreachably high windows, grandly dramatic doors that opened onto monklike cells or empty shafts, incredible upside-down staircases with upside-down treads and balustrades.

Other staircases, clinging airily to the side of a monumental wall, petered out after two or three landings, in the high gloom of the cupolas, arriving nowhere. I cannot say whether these are literal examples I have given; I do know that for many years they plagued my troubled dreams; I can no longer know whether any given feature is a faithful transcription of reality or one of the shapes unleashed by my nights. *This City*, I thought, *is so horrific that its mere existence, the mere fact of its having endured—even in the middle of a secret desert—pollutes the past and the future and somehow compromises the stars. So long as this City endures, no one in the world can ever be happy or courageous.* I do not want to describe it; a chaos of heterogeneous words, the body of a tiger or a bull pullulating with teeth, organs, and heads monstrously yoked together yet hating each other—those might, perhaps, be approximate images.

I cannot recall the stages by which I returned, nor my path through the dusty, humid crypts. I know only that I was accompanied by the constant fear that when I emerged from the last labyrinth I would be surrounded once again by the abominable City of the Immortals. I remember nothing else. That loss of memory, now insurmountable, was perhaps willful; it is possible that the circumstances of my escape were so unpleasant that on some day no less lost to memory I swore to put them out of my mind.

III

Those who have read the story of my travails attentively will recall that a man of the Troglodyte tribe had followed me, as a dog might have, into the jagged shadow of the walls. When I emerged from the last cellar, I found him at the mouth of the cavern. He was lying in the sand, clumsily drawing and rubbing out a row of symbols that resembled those letters in dreams that one is just on the verge of understanding when they merge and blur. At first I thought that this was some sort of barbaric writing; then I realized that it was absurd to imagine that men who had never learned to speak should have invented writing. Nor did any one of the shapes resemble any other—a fact that ruled out (or made quite remote) the possibility that they were symbols. The man would draw them, look at them, and correct them. Then suddenly, as though his game irritated him, he would rub them out with his palm and forearm. He looked up at me, though he seemed not to recognize me. Still, so great was the relief I felt (or so great, so dreadful had my loneliness been) that I actually thought that this primitive Troglodyte looking up at me from the floor of a cave had been waiting for me. The sun warmed the plain; as we began our return to the village, under the first stars of evening, the sand burned our feet. The Troglodyte walked ahead of me; that night I resolved to teach him to recognize, perhaps even to repeat, a few words. Dogs and horses, I reflected, are able to do the first; many birds, like the Cæsars' nightingale, can do the second. However scant a man's understanding, it will always be greater than that of unreasoning beasts.

The Troglodyte's lowly birth and condition recalled to my memory the image of Argos, the moribund old dog of the *Odyssey*, so I gave him the name Argos, and tried to teach it to him. Time and time again, I failed. No means I employed, no severity, no obstinacy of mine availed. Motionless, his eyes dead, he seemed not even to perceive the sounds which I was attempting to imprint upon him. Though but a few paces from me, he seemed immensely distant. Lying in the sand like a small, battered sphinx carved from lava, he allowed the heavens to circle in the sky above him from the first dusky light of morning to the last dusky light of night. It seemed simply impossible that he had not grasped my intention. I recalled that it is generally believed among the Ethiopians that monkeys deliberately do not speak, so that they will not be forced to work; I attributed Argos' silence to distrust or fear. From that vivid picture I passed on to others, even more extravagant. I reflected that Argos and I lived our lives in separate universes; I reflected that our perceptions were identical but that Argos combined them differently than I, constructed from them different objects; I reflected that perhaps for him there were no objects, but rather a constant, dizzying play of swift impressions. I imagined a world without memory, without time; I toyed with the possibility of a language that had no nouns, a language of impersonal verbs or indeclinable adjectives. In these reflections many days went by, and with the days, years. Until one morning, something very much like joy occurred—the sky rained slow, strong rain.

Nights in the desert can be frigid, but that night had been like a cauldron. I dreamed that a river in Thessaly (into whose waters I had thrown back a golden fish) was coming to save me; I could hear it approaching over the red sand and the black rock; a coolness in the air and the scurrying sound of rain awakened me. I ran out naked to welcome it. The night was waning; under the yellow clouds, the tribe, as joyously as I, was offering itself up to the vivid torrents in a kind of ecstasy—they reminded me of Corybantes possessed by the god. Argos, his eyes fixed on the empyrean, was moaning; streams of water rolled down his face— not just rain, but also (I later learned) tears. *Argos*, I cried, *Argos!*

Then, with gentle wonder, as though discovering something lost and forgotten for many years, Argos stammered out these words: *Argos, Ulysses' dog*. And then, without looking at me, *This dog lying on the dungheap*.

We accept reality so readily—perhaps because we sense that nothing is real. I asked Argos how much of the *Odyssey* he knew. He found using Greek difficult; I had to repeat the question.

Very little, he replied. *Less than the meagerest rhapsode. It has been eleven hundred years since last I wrote it.*

IV

That day, all was revealed to me. The Troglodytes were the Immortals; the stream and its sand-laden waters, the River sought by the rider. As for the City whose renown had spread to the very Ganges, the Immortals had destroyed it almost nine hundred years ago. Out of the shattered remains of the City's ruin they had built on the same spot the incoherent city I had wandered through— that parody or antithesis of City which was also a temple to the irrational gods that rule the world and to those gods about whom we know nothing save that they do not resemble man. The founding of this city was the last symbol to which the Immortals had descended; it marks the point at which, esteeming all exertion vain, they resolved to live in thought, in pure speculation. They built that carapace, abandoned it, and went off to make their dwellings in the caves. In their self-absorption, they scarcely perceived the physical world.

These things were explained to me by Homer as one might explain things to a child. He also told me of his own old age and of that late journey he had made—driven, like Ulysses, by the intention to arrive at the nation of men that know not what the sea is, that eat not salted meat, that know not what an oar might be. He lived for a century in the City of the Immortals, and when it was destroyed it was he who counseled that this other one be built. We should not be surprised by that—it is rumored that after singing of the war of Ilion, he sang of the war between the frogs and rats. He was like a god who created first the Cosmos, and then Chaos.

There is nothing very remarkable about being immortal; with the exception of mankind, all creatures are immortal, for they know nothing of death. What is divine, terrible, and incomprehensible is *to know* oneself immortal. I have noticed that in spite of religion, the conviction as to one's own immortality is extraordinarily rare. Jews, Christians, and Muslims all *profess* belief in immortality, but the veneration paid to the first century of life is proof that they truly believe only in those hundred years, for they destine all the rest, throughout eternity, to rewarding or punishing what one did *when alive*. In my view, the Wheel conceived by certain religions in Hindustan is much more plausible; on that Wheel, which has neither end nor beginning, each life is the effect of the previous life and engenderer of the next, yet no one life determines the whole. . . .Taught by centuries of living, the republic of immortal men had achieved a perfection of tolerance, almost of disdain. They knew that over an infinitely long span of time, all things happen to all men. As reward for his past and future virtues, every man merited every kindness—yet also every betrayal, as reward for his past and future iniquities. Much as the way in games of chance, heads and tails tend to even out, so cleverness and dullness cancel and correct each other. Perhaps the rude poem of El Cid is the counterweight demanded by a single epithet of the Eclogues or a maxim from Heraclitus. The most fleeting thought obeys an invisible plan, and may crown, or inaugurate, a secret design. I know of men who have done evil in order that good may come of it in future centuries, or may already have come of it in centuries past. . . .Viewed in that way, all our acts are just, though also unimportant. There are no spiritual or intellectual *merits*. Homer composed the *Odyssey*; given infinite time, with infinite circumstances and changes, it is impossible that the *Odyssey* should *not* be composed at least once. No one is someone; a single immortal man is all men. Like Cornelius Agrippa, I am god, hero, philosopher, demon, and world—which is a long-winded way of saying that *I am not*.

The notion of the world as a system of exact compensations had an enormous influence on the Immortals. In the first place, it made them immune to pity. I have mentioned the ancient quarries that dotted the countryside on the far bank of the stream; a man fell into the deepest of those pits; he could not be hurt, could not die, and yet he burned with thirst; seventy years passed before he was thrown a rope. Nor was he much interested in his own fate. His body was a submissive domestic animal; all the charity it required each month was a few hours' sleep, a little water, and a scrap of meat. But let no one imagine that we were mere ascetics. There is no more complex pleasure than thought, and it was to thought that we delivered ourselves over. From time to time, some extraordinary stimulus might bring us back to the physical world—for example, on that dawn, the ancient elemental pleasure of the rain. But those lapses were extremely rare; all Immortals were capable of perfect quietude. I recall one whom I never saw standing—a bird had made its nest on his breast.

Among the corollaries to the doctrine that there is no thing that is not counterbalanced by another, there is one that has little theoretical importance but that caused us, at the beginning or end of the tenth century, to scatter over the face of the earth. It may be summarized in these words: *There is a river whose waters give immortality; somewhere there must be another river whose waters take it away.* The number of rivers is not infinite; an immortal traveler wandering the world will someday have drunk from them all. We resolved to find that river.

Death (or reference to death) makes men precious and pathetic; their ghostliness is touching; any act they perform may be their last; there is no face that is not on the verge of blurring and fading away like the faces in a dream. Everything in the world of mortals has the value of the irrecoverable and contingent. Among the Immortals, on the other hand, every act (every thought) is the echo of others that preceded it in the past, with no visible beginning, and the faithful presage of others that will repeat it in the future, *ad vertiginem*. There is nothing that is not as though lost between indefatigable mirrors. Nothing can occur but once, nothing is preciously *in peril of being lost*. The elegiac, the somber, the ceremonial are not modes the Immortals hold in reverence. Homer and I went our separate ways at the portals of Tangier; I do not think we said good-bye.

V

I wandered through new realms, new empires. In the autumn of 1066 I fought at Stamford Bridge, though I no longer recall whether I stood in the ranks of Harold, soon to meet his fate, or in the ranks of that ill-fated Harald Hardrada who conquered only six feet or a little more of English soil. In the seventh century of the Hegira, on the outskirts of Bulaq, I transcribed with deliberate calligraphy, in a language I have forgotten, in an alphabet I know not, the seven voyages of Sindbad and the story of the City of Brass. In a courtyard of the prison in Samarkand I often played chess. In Bikanir I have taught astrology, as I have in Bohemia. In 1638 I was in Kolzsvar, and later in Leipzig. In Aberdeen, in 1714, I subscribed to the six volumes of Pope's *Iliad*; I know I often perused them with delight. In 1729 or thereabouts, I discussed the origin of that poem with a professor of rhetoric whose name, I believe, was Giambattista; his arguments struck me as irrefutable. On October 4, 1921, the *Patna*, which was taking me to Bombay, ran aground in a harbor on the Eritrean coast.[1] I disembarked; there came to my mind other mornings, long in the past, when I had also looked out over the Red Sea—when I was a Roman tribune, and fever and magic and inactivity consumed the soldiers. Outside the city I saw a spring; impelled by habit, I tasted its clear water. As I scaled the steep bank beside it, a thorny tree scratched the back of my hand. The unaccustomed pain seemed exceedingly sharp. Incredulous, speechless, and in joy, I contemplated the precious formation of a slow drop of blood. *I am once more mortal*, I told myself over and over, *again I am like all other men*. That night, I slept until daybreak.

1. Part of the ms. is scratched out just here; the name of the port may have been erased.

. . . A year has passed, and I reread these pages. I can attest that they do not stray beyond the bounds of truth, although in the first chapters, and even in certain paragraphs of others, I believe I detect a certain falseness. That is due, perhaps, to an overemployment of circumstantial details, a way of writing that I learned from poets; it is a procedure that infects everything with falseness, since there may be a wealth of details in the event, yet not in memory. . . .I believe, nonetheless, that I have discovered a more private and inward reason. I will reveal it; it does not matter that I may be judged a fantast.

The story I have told seems unreal because the experiences of two different men are intermingled in it. In the first chapter, the horseman wishes to know the name of the river that runs beside the walls of Thebes; Flaminius Rufus, who had bestowed upon the city the epithet "hundred-gated," tells him that the river is the "Egypt"; neither of those statements belongs to *him*, but rather to Homer, who in the *Iliad* expressly mentions "Thebes Hekatompylos" and who in the *Odyssey*, through the mouths of Proteus and Ulysses, invariably calls the Nile the "Egypt." In the second chapter, when the Roman drinks the immortal water he speaks a few words in Greek. Those words are also Homeric; they may be found at the end of the famous catalog of the ships. Later, in the dizzying palace, he speaks of "a reproof that was almost remorse"; those words, too, belong to Homer, who had foreseen such a horror. Such anomalies disturbed me; others, of an æsthetic nature, allowed me to discover the truth. The clues of this latter type may be found in the last chapter, which says that I fought at Stamford Bridge, that in Bulaq I transcribed the voyages of Sindbad the Sailor, and that in Aberdeen I subscribed to Pope's English *Iliad*. The text says, *inter alia*: "In Bikanir I have taught astrology, as I have in Bohemia." None of those statements is false; what is significant is the fact of their having been chosen to record. The first seems to befit a man of war, but then one sees that the narrator pays little attention to the war, much more to the fate of the men. The "facts" that follow are even more curious. A dark yet elemental reason led me to put them to paper: I knew they were pathetic. They are not pathetic when narrated by the Roman Flaminius Rufus; they are when narrated by Homer. It is odd that Homer, in the thirteenth century, should have copied down the adventures of Sindbad—another Ulysses—and again after many hundreds of years have discovered forms like those of his own *Iliad* in a northern kingdom and a barbaric tongue. As for the sentence that contains the name "Bikanir," one can see that it has been composed by a man of letters desirous (like the author of the catalog of ships) of wielding splendid words.[1]

As the end approaches, there are no longer any images from memory—there are only words. It is not strange that time may have confused those that once portrayed *me* with those that were symbols of the fate of *the person that accompanied me for so many centuries.* I have been Homer; soon, like Ulysses, I shall be Nobody; soon, I shall be all men—I shall be dead.

Postscript (1950): Among the commentaries inspired by the foregoing publication, the most curious (if not most urbane) is biblically titled *A Coat of Many Colours* (Manchester, 1948); it is the work of the supremely perseverant pen of Dr. Nahum Cordovero, and contains some hundred pages. It speaks of the Greek anthologies, of the anthologies of late Latin texts, of that Ben Johnson who defined his contemporaries with excerpts from Seneca, of Alexander Ross's *Virgilius evangelizans,* of the artifices of George Moore and Eliot, and, finally, of "the tale attributed to the rare-book dealer Joseph Cartaphilus." In the first chapter it points out brief interpolations from Pliny (*Historia naturalis,* V:8); in the

---

[1]. Ernesto Sabato suggests that the "Giambattista" who discussed the origins of the *Iliad* with the rare book dealer Cartaphilus is Giambattista Vico, the Italian who defended the argument that Homer is a symbolic character, like Pluto or Achilles.

second, from Thomas de Quincey (*Writings*, III: 439); in the third, from a letter written by Descartes to the ambassador Pierre Chanut; in the fourth, from Bernard Shaw (*Back to Methuselah*, V). From those "intrusions" (or thefts) it infers that the entire document is apocryphal.

To my way of thinking, that conclusion is unacceptable. *As the end approaches*, wrote Cartaphilus, *there are no longer any images from memory—there are only words.* Words, words, words taken out of place and mutilated, words from other men—those were the alms left him by the hours and the centuries.

For Cecilia Ingenieros

The Dead Man

That a man from the outskirts of Buenos Aires, a sad sort of hoodlum whose only recommendation was his infatuation with courage, should go out into the wilderness of horse country along the Brazilian frontier and become a leader of a band of smugglers—such a thing would, on the face of it, seem impossible. For those who think so, I want to tell the story of the fate of Benjamín Otálora, whom no one may remember anymore in the neighborhood of Balvanera but who died as he lived, by a bullet, in the province of Rio Grande do Sul.* I do not know the full details of his adventure; when I am apprised of them, I will correct and expand these pages. For now, this summary may be instructive:

In 1891, Benjamín Otálora is nineteen years old—a strapping young man with a miserly brow, earnest blue eyes, and the strength and stamina of a Basque. A lucky knife thrust has revealed to him that he is a man of courage; he is not distressed by the death of his opponent, or by the immediate need to flee the country. The ward boss of his parish gives him a letter of introduction to a man named Azevedo Bandeira, over in Uruguay. Otálora takes ship; the crossing is stormy, creaking; the next day finds him wandering aimlessly through the streets of Montevideo, with unconfessed and perhaps unrecognized sadness. He doesn't manage to come across Azevedo Bandeira. Toward midnight, in a general-store-and-bar in Paso del Molino,* he witnesses a fight between two cattle drovers. A knife gleams; Otálora doesn't know whose side he should be on, but he is attracted by the pure taste of danger, the way other men are attracted by gambling or music. In the confusion, he checks a low thrust meant for a man in a broad-brimmed black hat and a poncho. That man later turns out to be Azevedo Bandeira. (When Otálora discovers this, he tears up the letter of introduction, because he'd rather all the credit be his alone.) Though Azevedo Bandeira is a strong, well-built man, he gives the unjustifiable impression of being something of a fake, a forgery. In his face (which is always too close) there mingle the Jew, the Negro, and the Indian; in his air, the monkey and the tiger; the scar that crosses his face is just another piece of decoration, like the bristling black mustache.

Whether it's a projection or an error caused by drink, the fight stops as quickly as it started. Otálora drinks with the cattle drovers and then goes out carousing with them and then accompanies them to a big house in the Old City—by now the sun is high in the sky. Out in the back patio, the men lay out their bedrolls. Otálora vaguely compares that night with the previous one; now he is on terra firma, among friends. He does, he has to admit, feel a small twinge of remorse at not missing Buenos Aires. He sleeps till orisons, when he is awakened by the same *paisano* who had drunkenly attacked Bandeira. (Otálora recalls that this man has been with the others, drunk with them, made the rounds of the city with them, that Bandeira sat him at his right hand and made him keep drinking.) The man tells him the boss wants to see him. In a kind of office that opens off the long entryway at the front of the house (Otálora has never seen an entryway with doors opening off it), Azevedo Bandeira is waiting for him, with a splendid, contemptuous red-haired woman. Bandeira heaps praise on Otálora, offers him a glass of harsh brandy, tells him again that he looks like a man of mettle, and asks him if he'd like to go up north with the boys to bring a herd back. Otálora takes the job; by dawn the next morning they are on their way to Tacuarembó.

That is the moment at which Otálora begins a new life, a life of vast sunrises and days that smell of horses. This life is new to him, and sometimes terrible, and yet it is in his blood, for just as the men of other lands worship the sea and can feel it deep inside them, the men of ours (including the man who weaves these symbols) yearn for the inexhaustible plains that echo under the horses' hooves. Otálora has been brought up in neighborhoods full of cart drivers and leather braiders; within a year, he has become a gaucho. He learns to ride, to keep the horses together, to butcher the animals, to use the rope that lassos them and the bolas that bring them down, to bear up under weariness, storms, cold weather, and the sun, to herd the animals with whistles and shouts. Only once during this period of apprenticeship does he see Azevedo Bandeira, but he is always aware of his presence, because to be a "Bandeira man" is to be taken seriously—in fact, to be feared—and because no matter the deed of manly strength or courage they see done, the gauchos say Bandeira does it better. One of them says he thinks Bandeira was born on the other side of the Cuareim, in Rio Grande do Sul; that fact, which ought to bring him down a notch or two in their estimation, lends his aura a vague new wealth of teeming forests, swamps, impenetrable and almost infinite distances.

Gradually, Otálora realizes that Bandeira has many irons in the fire, and that his main business is smuggling. Being a drover is being a servant; Otálora decides to rise higher—decides to become a smuggler. One night, two of his companions are to cross the border to bring back several loads of brandy; Otálora provokes one of them, wounds him, and takes his place. He is moved by ambition, but also by an obscure loyalty. *Once and for all* (he thinks) *I want the boss to see that I'm a better man than all these Uruguayans of his put together.*

Another year goes by before Otálora returns to Montevideo. They ride through the outskirts, and then through the city (which seems enormous to Otálora); they come to the boss's house; the men lay out their bedrolls in the back patio. Days go by, and Otálora hasn't seen Bandeira. They say, timorously, that he's sick; a black man takes the kettle and *mate* up to him in his room. One afternoon, Otálora is asked to carry the things up to Bandeira. He feels somehow humiliated by this, but derives some pride from it, too.

The bedroom is dark and shabby. There is a balcony facing west, a long table with a gleaming jumble of quirts and bullwhips, cinches, firearms, and knives, a distant mirror of cloudy glass. Bandeira is lying on his back, dozing and moaning some; a vehemence of last sunlight spotlights him. The vast white bed makes him seem smaller, and somehow dimmer; Otálora notes the gray hairs, the weariness, the slackness, and the lines of age. It suddenly galls him that it's this old man that's giving them their orders. One thrust, he thinks, would be enough to settle *that* matter. Just then, he sees in the mirror that someone has come into the room. It is the redheaded woman; she is barefoot and half dressed, and staring at him with cold curiosity. Bandeira sits up; while he talks about things out on the range and sips *mate* after *mate*, his fingers toy with the woman's hair. Finally, he gives Otálora leave to go.

Days later, they receive the order to head up north again. They come to a godforsaken ranch somewhere (that could be anywhere) in the middle of the unending plains. Not a tree, not a stream of water soften the place; the sun beats down on it from first light to last. There are stone corrals for the stock, which is long-horned and poorly. The miserable place is called *El Suspiro*—The Sigh.

Otálora hears from the peons that Bandeira will be coming up from Montevideo before long. He asks why, and somebody explains that there's a foreigner, a would-be gaucho type, that's getting too big for his britches. Otálora takes this as a joke, but he's flattered that the joke is possible. He later finds out that Bandeira has had a falling-out with some politico and the politico has withdrawn his protection. The news pleases Otálora.

Crates of firearms begin to arrive; a silver washbowl and pitcher arrive for the woman's bedroom, then curtains of elaborately figured damask; one morning a somber-faced rider with a thick beard and a poncho rides down from up in the mountains. His name is Ulpiano Suárez, and he is Azevedo Bandeira's *capanga*, his foreman. He talks very little, and there is something Brazilian about his speech when he does. Otálora doesn't know whether to attribute the man's reserve to hostility, contempt, or mere savagery, but he does know that for the plan he has in mind he has to win his friendship.

At this point there enters into Benjamín Otálora's life a sorrel with black feet, mane, and muzzle. Azevedo Bandeira brings the horse up with him from the south; its bridle and all its other gear is tipped with silver and the bindings on its saddle are of jaguar skin. That extravagant horse is a symbol of the boss's authority, which is why the youth covets it, and why he also comes to covet, with grudge-filled desire, the woman with the resplendent hair. The woman, the gear, and the sorrel are attributes (adjectives) of a man he hopes to destroy.

Here, the story grows deeper and more complicated. Azevedo Bandeira is accomplished in the art of progressive humiliation, the satanic ability to humiliate his interlocutor little by little, step by step, with a combination of truths and evasions; Otálora decides to employ that same ambiguous method for the hard task he has set himself. He decides that he will gradually push Azevedo Bandeira out of the picture. Through days of common danger he manages to win Suárez' friendship. He confides his plan to him, and Suárez promises to help. Many things happen after this, some of which I know about: Otálora doesn't obey Bandeira; he keeps forgetting, improving his orders, even turning them upside down. The universe seems to conspire with him, and things move very fast. One noon, there is a shoot-out with men from Rio Grande do Sul on the prairies bordering the Tacuarembó. Otálora usurps Bandeira's place and gives the Uruguayans orders. He is shot in the shoulder, but that afternoon Otálora goes back to *El Suspiro* on the boss's sorrel and that afternoon a few drops of his blood stain the jaguar skin and that night he sleeps with the woman with the shining hair. Other versions change the order of these events and even deny that they all occurred on a single day.

Though Bandeira is still nominally the boss, he gives orders that aren't carried out; Benjamín Otálora never touches him, out of a mixture of habit and pity.

The last scene of the story takes place during the excitement of the last night of 1894. That night, the men of *El Suspiro* eat fresh-butchered lamb and drink bellicose liquor. Somebody is infinitely strumming at a milonga that he has some difficulty playing. At the head of the table, Otálora, drunk, builds exultancy upon exultancy, jubilation upon jubilation; that vertiginous tower is a symbol of his inexorable fate. Bandeira, taciturn among the boisterous men, lets the night take its clamorous course. When the twelve strokes of the clock chime at last, he stands up like a man remembering an engagement. He stands up and knocks softly on the woman's door. She opens it immediately, as though she were waiting for the knock. She comes out barefoot and half dressed. In an effeminate, wheedling voice, the boss speaks an order:

"Since you and the city slicker there are so in love, go give him a kiss so everybody can see."

He adds a vulgar detail. The woman tries to resist, but two men have taken her by the arms, and they throw her on top of Otálora. In tears, she kisses his face and his chest. Ulpiano Suárez has pulled his gun. Otálora realizes, before he dies, that he has been betrayed from the beginning, that he has been sentenced to death, that he has been allowed to love, to command, and win because he was already as good as dead, because so far as Bandeira was concerned, he was already a dead man.

Suárez fires, almost with a sneer.

The Theologians

The gardens ravaged, the altars and chalices profaned, the Huns rode their horses into the monastery library and mangled the incomprehensible books and reviled and burned them—fearful perhaps that the letters of the books might harbor blasphemies against their god, which was a scimitar of iron. They burned palimpsests and codices, but in the heart of the bonfire, among the ashes, there lay, virtually untouched by the flames, the twelfth book of the *Civitas Dei*, which says that in Athens Plato once taught that at the end of time all things will return again to where they once were—that he, in Athens, before the same circle of listeners, will one day teach that doctrine once again. That text spared by the flames came to enjoy a special veneration; those who read and reread it in that remote province came to forget that the author put forth the doctrine only in order more roundly to refute it. A hundred years later, Aurelian, bishop-coadjutor of Aquileia, learned that on the banks of the Danube the newborn sect called the *Monotoni* (also the *Annulari*) was claiming that history is a circle, and that all things that exist have existed before and will exist again. In the mountains, the Wheel and the Serpent had supplanted the Cross. Fear gripped all men's hearts, yet all were comforted by the rumor that John of Pannonia, who had distinguished himself by a treatise on the seventh attribute of God, was preparing to refute this abominable heresy.

Aurelian deplored the entire situation—especially this last report. He knew that in theology, there is no novelty without danger; then he reflected that the notion of circular time was too strange, too shocking, for the danger to be very serious. (The heresies we ought to fear are those that can be confused with orthodoxy.) He was pained most of all by the intervention—the intrusion—of John of Pannonia. Two years before, John's verbose treatise *De septima affectione Dei sive de æternitate* had trespassed upon Aurelian's own field of expertise; now, as though the problem of time were his alone, John promised to set the *Annulari* right (no doubt with arguments befitting Procrustes, and remedies more terrible than the Serpent itself). . . . That night, Aurelian turned the pages of Plutarch's ancient dialogue on the ceasing of the oracles; in paragraph twenty-nine, he read a gibe against the Stoics, who defended the idea of an infinite cycle of worlds, with infinite suns, moons, Apollos, Artemisias, and Poseidons. His coming upon this passage was a good omen; he resolved to steal a march on John of Pannonia and refute the heretics of the Wheel himself.

There are those who seek the love of a woman in order to stop thinking of her, to put her out of their mind; similarly, Aurelian wanted to outstrip John of Pannonia not because he wished to do him any harm, but in order to cure himself of the grudge he held for the man. His temper cooled by mere labor, by the crafting of syllogisms and the invention of contumely, by the *nego*'s and *autem*'s and *nequaquam*'s, the rancor dropped away. He constructed vast labyrinthine periods, made impassable by the piling-up of clauses upon clauses—clauses in which oversight and bad grammar seemed manifestations of disdain. He crafted an instrument from cacophony. He foresaw that John would thunder down on the Annulari with the gravity of a prophet; resolved to come at the problem from a different tack, he himself chose derision. Augustine had written that Jesus was the straight path that leads men out of the circular labyrinth in which the impious wander; Aurelian, in his painstakingly trivial way, compared the impious with Ixion, with Prometheus' liver, with Sisyphus, with that king of Thebes who saw two suns, with stuttering, with parrots, mirrors, echoes, mules chained to treadmills, and two-horned syllogisms. (The heathen fables had managed to endure, though reduced now to decoration.) Like all those who possess libraries, Aurelian felt a nagging sense of guilt at not being acquainted with every volume in his; this controversy allowed him to read many of the books that had seemed to reproach his neglect. Thus it was that he inserted into his text a passage from Origen's *De principiis* in which Origen denies that Judas Iscariot will sell the Lord again, that Paul will once more witness Stephen's martyrdom in Jerusalem, and another passage from Cicero's *Academica priora* in which Cicero mocks those who dream that while Cicero is speaking with Lucullus, other Luculluses and other Ciceros, infinite in number, speak precisely the same words in infinite identical worlds. He also scourged the Monotoni with that text from Plutarch on the obsolescence of the oracles, and decried the scandalous fact that the *lumen naturæ* should mean more to an idolater than the word of God to the Monotoni. The labor of composition took Aurelian nine days; on the tenth, he received a copy of the refutation written by John of Pannonia.

It was almost ludicrously brief; Aurelian looked at it with contempt, and then with foreboding. The first section glossed the closing verses of the ninth chapter of the Epistle to the Hebrews, which say that Jesus has not suffered many times since the foundation of the world, but has been sacrificed now, once, "in the end of the world." The second section cited the biblical injunction concerning the "vain repetitions" of the heathens (Matthew 6:7) and that passage from the seventh book of Pliny which praises the fact that in all the wide universe there are no two faces that are the same. John of Pannonia declared that no two souls were the same, either, and that the basest sinner is as precious as the blood shed for him by Jesus Christ. The act of a single man, he said, weighs more than the nine concentric heavens, and to think, erroneously, that it can be lost and then return again is naught but spectacular foolishness. Time does not restore what we lose; eternity holds it for glory, and also for the fire. John's treatise was limpid, universal; it seemed written not by a particular person, but by any man—or perhaps all men.

Aurelian felt an almost physical sense of humiliation. He considered destroying or reworking his own manuscript; then, with grudging honesty, he sent it off to Rome without changing a letter. Months later, when the Council of Pergamo was convened, the theologian entrusted with refuting the errors of the Monotoni was (predictably) John of Pannonia; his learnèd, measured refutation was the argument that condemned the heresiarch Euphorbus to the stake. *This has occurred once, and will occur again*, said Euphorbus. *It is not one pyre you are lighting, it is a labyrinth of fire. If all the fires on which I have been burned were brought together here, the earth would be too small for them, and the angels would be blinded. These words I have spoken many times.* Then he screamed, for the flames had engulfed him.

The Wheel fell to the Cross,[1] but the secret battle between John and Aurelian continued. The two men were soldiers in the same army, strove for the same prize, fought against the same Enemy, yet Aurelian wrote not a word that was not aimed, however unconfessably, at besting John. Their duel was an invisible one; if I may trust the swollen indices of Migne's *Patrology*, not once does *the other man's name* figure in the many volumes of Aurelian's works collected therein for posterity. (Of John's writings, only twenty words have survived.) Both men deplored the anathemas of the second Council of Constantinople; both persecuted the Arians, who denied the eternal generation of the Son; both attested to the orthodoxy of Cosmas' *Topographia christiana*, which taught that the earth is foursquare, like the Jewish tabernacle. Then, unfortunately, another tempestuous heresy spread to those four corners of the earth. Spawned in Egypt or in

1. In Runic crosses the two enemy emblems coexist, intertwined.

Asia (for accounts differ, and Bousset refuses to accept Harnack's arguments), the sect soon infested the eastern provinces, and sanctuaries were built in Macedonia, Carthage, and Trèves. It seemed to be everywhere; people said that in the diocese of Britain crucifixes had been turned upside down and in Cæsaria the image of the Lord had been supplanted by a mirror. The mirror and the obolus were the emblems of these new schismatics.

History knows them by many names (*Speculari, Abysmali, Cainitæ*), but the most widely accepted is *Histrioni*, the name that Aurelian gave them and that they defiantly adopted for themselves. In Phrygia, they were called the *Simulacra*, and in Dardania as well. John of Damascus called them "*Forms*"; it seems only right to point out that Erfjord thinks the passage apocryphal. There is no heresiologue who does not express shock as he recounts their wild customs. Many Histrioni professed asceticism; some mutilated themselves, like Origen; others lived underground, in the sewers; others put out their own eyes; still others (the *Nebuchadnezzars* of Nitria) "grazed on grasses like the oxen, and their hair grew like the eagle's." From mortification and severity, they sometimes graduated to crime; certain communities tolerated theft; others, homicide; others, sodomy, incest, and bestiality. All were blasphemous; they cursed not only the Christian God, but even the arcane deities of their own pantheon. They plotted together to write sacred texts, whose disappearance is a great loss to scholars. In 1658, Sir Thomas Browne wrote the following: "Time has annihilated the ambitious *Histrionic* Gospels, although not so the Insultes with which their Impiousness was scourged"; Erfjord has suggested that those "insultes" (preserved in a Greek codex) are themselves the lost gospels. Unless we recall the Histrionic cosmology, such a suggestion is incomprehensible.

In the hermetic books, it is written that "things below are as things above, and things above as things below"; the Zohar tells us that the lower world is a reflection of the higher. The Histrioni founded their doctrine on a perversion of this idea. They invoked

Matthew 6:12 ("forgive us our debts, as we forgive our debtors")
and 11:12 ("the kingdom of heaven suffereth violence") to prove
that the earth influences heaven; they cited I Corinthians 13:12 ("For
now we see through a glass, darkly") to prove that all things we see
are false. Contaminated perhaps by the Monotoni, they imagined
that every man is two men, and that the real one is the *other* one, the
one in heaven. They also imagined that our acts cast an inverted
reflection, so that if we are awake, the other man is asleep; if we
fornicate, the other man is chaste; if we steal, the other man is
generous. When we die, they believed, we shall join him and *be*
him. (Some echo of these doctrines continues to be heard in Bloy.)
Other Histrioni believed that the world would end when the
number of its possibilities was exhausted; since there can be no
repetitions, the righteous are duty-bound to eliminate (commit) the
most abominable acts so that those acts will not sully the future and
so that the coming of the kingdom of Jesus may be hastened.

That particular article of faith was denied by other sects, which
rejoined that the history of the world must be acted out in
every man. Most men, like Pythagoras, will have to transmigrate
through many bodies before obtaining their liberation; some, the
Proteans, "within the period of a single life are lions, dragons,
wild boars, are water and are a tree." Demosthenes tells of the
purification by mud to which initiates were subjected as part of the
Orphic mysteries; analogously, the Proteans sought purification
through evil. It was their belief, as it was Carpocrates', that no
one shall emerge from the prison until the last obolus is paid
(Luke 12:59: "I tell thee, thou shalt not depart thence, till thou
hast paid the very last mite"), and they often hornswoggled
penitents with this other verse: "I am come that they might have
life, and that they might have it more abundantly" (John 10:10).
They also said that *not* to be an evildoer was an act of satanic
arrogance. . . .The Histrioni wove many, and diverse, mythologies; some preached asceticism, others license—all preached
confusion. Theopompus, a Histrion from Berenice, denied all

fables; he said that every man is an organ projected by the deity in order to perceive the world.

The heretics in Aurelian's diocese were not those who claimed that every act is reflected in heaven but rather those who claimed that time does not tolerate repetitions. The circumstance was peculiar; in a report to the authorities at Rome, Aurelian mentioned it. The prelate who received the report was the empress's confessor; everyone knew that this demanding minister forbade her the private delectations of speculative theology. His secretary— formerly one of John of Pannonia's collaborators, now fallen out with him—was famed as a most diligent inquisitor of hetero-doxies; Aurelian added an explanation of the Histrionic heresy, as it was contained in the conventicles of Genoa and Aquileia. He wrote a few paragraphs; when he tried to write the horrible thesis that no two moments are the same, his pen halted. He could not find the necessary words; the admonitions of the new doctrine were too affected and metaphorical to be transcribed. ("Wouldst thou see what no human eyes have seen? Look upon the moon. Wouldst thou hear what no ears have heard? Hearken to the cry of the bird. Wouldst thou touch what no hands have touched? Put thy hand to the earth. Verily I say unto thee, that the moment of God's creation of the world is yet to come.") Then suddenly a sentence of twenty words came to his spirit. With joy he wrote it on the page; immediately afterward, he was disturbed by the sense that it was someone else's. The next day, he remembered: he had read it many years ago in the *Adversus Annulares*, composed by John of Pannonia. He ferreted out the quotation—there it was. He was torn by uncertainty. To alter or omit those words was to weaken the force of the statement; to let them stand was to plagiarize a man he detested; to indicate the source was to denounce him. He pleaded for divine aid. Toward the coming of the second twilight, his guardian angel suggested a middle way. Aurelian kept the words, but set this disclaimer before it: *That which the heresiarchs howl today, to the confusion of the faith, was said during this century, with more levity than blameworthiness, by a most learnèd doctor of the church.* Then there occurred the thing he had feared, the thing he had hoped for, the thing that was inevitable. Aurelian was required to declare the identity of that doctor of the church; John of Pannonia was accused of professing heretical opinions.

Four months later, a blacksmith on the Aventinus, driven to delusions by the misrepresentations of the Histrioni, set a great iron ball upon the shoulders of his little son so that the child's double might fly. The man's child died; the horror engendered by the crime obliged John's judges to be irreproachably severe with him. The accused would not retract; time and again he repeated that to deny his proposition was to fall into the pestilential heresy of the Monotoni. He did not realize (perhaps *refused* to realize) that to speak of the Monotoni was to speak of a thing now forgotten. With somehow senile insistence, he poured forth the most brilliant periods of his old jeremiads; the judges did not even listen to what had once so shocked them. Rather than try to purify himself of the slightest stain of Histrionism, he redoubled his efforts to prove that the proposition of which he was accused was in fact utterly orthodox. He argued with the men upon whose verdict his very life depended, and he committed the supreme *faux pas* of doing so with genius and with sarcasm. On October 26, after a debate that had lasted three days and three nights, he was condemned to be burned at the stake.

Aurelian witnessed the execution, because to have avoided it would have been to confess himself responsible for it. The place of execution was a hill on whose summit stood a stake pounded deep into the ground; all around it, bundles of firewood had been gathered. A priest read the tribunal's verdict. Under the midday sun, John of Pannonia lay with his face in the dust, howling like a beast. He clawed at the ground, but the executioners seized him, stripped him, and tied him to the stake. On his head they put a crown of straw sprinkled with sulfur; beside him, a copy of the pestilential *Adversus Annulares*. It had rained the night before, and the wood burned smokily. John of Pannonia prayed in Greek, and then in an unknown language. The pyre was about to consume him, when Aurelian screwed up his courage to raise his eyes. The fiery gusts fell still; Aurelian saw for the first and last time the face of the man he hated. It reminded him of someone, but he couldn't quite remember whom. Then, the flames swallowed him; he screamed and it was as though the fire itself were screaming.

Plutarch reports that Julius Cæsar wept at the death of Pompey; Aurelian did not weep at the death of John, but he did feel what a man cured of an incurable disease that had become a part of his life might feel. In Aquileia, in Ephesus, in Macedonia, he let the years pass over him. He sought out the hard ends of the empire, the floundering swamps and the contemplative deserts, so that solitude might help him understand his life. In a Mauritanian cell, in the night laden with lions, he rethought the complex accusation against John of Pannonia and for the millionth time he justified the verdict. It was harder for him to justify his tortuous denunciation. In Rusaddir he preached that anachronistic sermon titled *The Light of Lights Lighted in the Flesh of a Reprobate.* In Hibernia, in one of the huts of a monastery besieged by forest, he was surprised one night, toward dawn, by the sound of rain. He recalled a Roman night when that same punctilious sound had surprised him. At high noon, a lighting bolt set the trees afire, and Aurelian died as John had.

The end of the story can only be told in metaphors, since it takes place in the kingdom of heaven, where time does not exist. One might say that Aurelian spoke with God and found that God takes so little interest in religious differences that He took him for John of Pannonia. That, however, would be to impute confusion to the divine intelligence. It is more correct to say that in paradise, Aurelian discovered that in the eyes of the unfathomable deity, he and John of Pannonia (the orthodox and the heretic, the abominator and the abominated, the accuser and the victim) were a single person.

Story of the Warrior and the Captive Maiden

On page 278 of his book *La poesia* (Bari, 1942), Croce, summarizing and shortening a Latin text by the historian Paul the Deacon, tells the story of the life of Droctulft and quotes his epitaph; I found myself remarkably moved by both life and epitaph, and later I came to understand why. Droctulft was a Lombard warrior who during the siege of Ravenna deserted his own army and died defending the city he had been attacking. The people of Ravenna buried him in a church sanctuary; they composed an epitaph in which they expressed their gratitude (CONTEMPSIT CAROS DUM NOS AMAT ILLE PARENTES) and remarked upon the singular contrast between the horrific figure of that barbarian and his simplicity and kindness:

TERRIBILIS VISU FACIES SED MENTE BENIGNUS,
  LONGAQUE ROBUSTO PECTORE BARBA FUIT[1]

Such is the story of the life of Droctulft, a barbarian who died defending Rome—or such is the fragment of his story that Paul the Deacon was able to preserve. I do not even know when the event occurred, whether in the mid-sixth century when the Longobards laid waste to the plains of Italy or in the eighth, before Ravenna's surrender. Let us imagine (this is not a work of history) that it was the mid-sixth century.

1. Gibbon also records these lines, in the *Decline and Fall*, Chapter XLV.

Let us imagine Droctulft *sub specie æternitatis*—not the individual Droctulft, who was undoubtedly unique and fathomless (as all individuals are), but rather the generic "type" that tradition (the work of memory and forgetting) has made of him and many others like him. Through a gloomy geography of swamps and forests, wars bring him from the shores of the Danube or the Elbe to Italy, and he may not realize that he is going toward the south, nor know that he is waging war against a thing called Rome. It is possible that his faith is that of the Arians, who hold that the glory of the Son is a mere reflection of the glory of the Father, but it seems more fitting to imagine him a worshiper of the earth, Hertha, whose veiled idol is borne from hut to hut in a cart pulled by cattle—or of the gods of war and thunder, who are crude wooden figures swathed in woven clothing and laden with coins and bangles. He comes from the dense forests of the wild boar and the urus; he is white, courageous, innocent, cruel, loyal to his captain and his tribe—not to the universe. Wars bring him to Ravenna, and there he sees something he has never seen before, or never fully seen. He sees daylight and cypresses and marble. He sees an aggregate that is multiple yet without disorder; he sees a city, an organism, composed of statues, temples, gardens, rooms, tiered seats, amphoræ, capitals and pediments, and regular open spaces. None of those artifices (I know this) strikes him as beautiful; they strike him as we would be struck today by a complex machine whose purpose we know not but in whose design we sense an immortal intelligence at work. Perhaps a single arch is enough for him, with its incomprehensible inscription of eternal Roman letters—he is suddenly blinded and renewed by the City, that revelation. He knows that in this city there will be a dog, or a child, and that he will not even begin to understand it, but he knows as well that this city is worth more than his gods and the faith he is sworn to and all the marshlands of Germany. Droctulft deserts his own kind and fights for Ravenna. He dies, and on his gravestone are carved words that he would not have understood:

CONTEMPSIT CAROS DUM NOS AMAT ILLE PARENTES,
HANC PATRIAM REPUTANS ESSE, RAVENNA, SUAM

Droctulft was not a traitor; traitors seldom inspire reverential epitaphs. He was an *illuminatus*, a convert. After many generations, the Longobards who had heaped blame upon the turncoat did as he had done; they became Italians, Lombards, and one of their number—Aldiger—may have fathered those who fathered Alighieri. . . .There are many conjectures one might make about Droctulft's action; mine is the most economical; if it is not true as fact, it may nevertheless be true as symbol.

When I read the story of this warrior in Croce's book, I found myself enormously moved, and I was struck by the sense that I was recovering, under a different guise, something that had once been my own. I fleetingly thought of the Mongol horsemen who had wanted to make China an infinite pastureland, only to grow old in the cities they had yearned to destroy; but that was not the memory I sought. I found it at last—it was a tale I had heard once from my English grandmother, who is now dead.

In 1872 my grandfather Borges was in charge of the northern and western borders of Buenos Aires province and the southern border of Santa Fe. The headquarters was in Junín; some four or five leagues farther on lay the chain of forts; beyond that, what was then called "the pampas" and also "the interior." One day my grandmother, half in wonder, half in jest, remarked upon her fate—an Englishwoman torn from her country and her people and carried to this far end of the earth. The person to whom she made the remark told her she wasn't the only one, and months later pointed out an Indian girl slowly crossing the town square. She was barefoot, and wearing two red ponchos; the roots of her hair were blond. A soldier told her that another Englishwoman wanted to talk with her. The woman nodded; she went into the headquarters without fear but not without some misgiving. Set in her coppery face painted with fierce colors, her eyes were that halfhearted blue that the English call gray. Her body was as light as a deer's; her hands, strong and bony. She had come in from the wilderness, from "the interior," and everything seemed too small for her—the doors, the walls, the furniture.

Perhaps for one instant the two women saw that they were sisters; they were far from their beloved island in an incredible land. My grandmother, enunciating carefully, asked some question or other; the other woman replied haltingly, searching for the words and then repeating them, as though astonished at the old taste of them. It must have been fifteen years since she'd spoken her native language, and it was not easy to recover it. She said she was from Yorkshire, that her parents had emigrated out to Buenos Aires, that she had lost them in an Indian raid, that she had been carried off by the Indians, and that now she was the wife of a minor chieftain—she'd given him two sons; he was very brave. She said all this little by little, in a clumsy sort of English interlarded with words from the Araucan or Pampas tongue*, and behind the tale one caught glimpses of a savage and uncouth life: tents of horsehide, fires fueled by dung, celebrations in which the people feasted on meat singed over the fire or on raw viscera, stealthy marches at dawn; the raid on the corrals, the alarm sounded, the plunder, the battle, the thundering roundup of the stock by naked horsemen, polygamy, stench, and magic. An Englishwoman, reduced to such barbarism! Moved by outrage and pity, my grandmother urged her not to go back. She swore to help her, swore to rescue her children. The other woman answered that she was happy, and she returned that night to the desert. Francisco Borges was to die a short time later, in the Revolution of '74; perhaps at that point my grandmother came to see that other woman, torn like herself from her own kind and transformed by that implacable continent, as a monstrous mirror of her own fate. . . .

Every year, that blond-haired Indian woman had come into

the *pulperías** in Junín or Fort Lavalle, looking for trinkets and "vices"; after the conversation with my grandmother, she never appeared again. But they did see each other one more time. My grandmother had gone out hunting; alongside a squalid hut near the swamplands, a man was slitting a sheep's throat. As though in a dream, the Indian woman rode by on horseback. She leaped to the ground and drank up the hot blood. I cannot say whether she did that because she was no longer capable of acting in any other way, or as a challenge, and a sign.

Thirteen hundred years and an ocean lie between the story of the life of the kidnapped maiden and the story of the life of Droctulft. Both, now, are irrecoverable. The figure of the barbarian who embraced the cause of Ravenna, and the figure of the European woman who chose the wilderness—they might seem conflicting, contradictory. But both were transported by some secret impulse, an impulse deeper than reason, and both embraced that impulse that they would not have been able to explain. It may be that the stories I have told are one and the same story. The obverse and reverse of this coin are, in the eyes of God, identical.

For Ulrike von Kühlmann

A Biography of Tadeo Isidoro Cruz
(1829–1874)

I'm looking for the face I had
Before the world was made.
   Yeats, *The Winding Stair*

On February 6, 1829, the *montoneros**—who by this time were being hounded by Lavalle*—were marching northward to join López' divisions; they halted at a ranch whose name they did not know, three or four leagues from the Pergamino. Toward dawn, one of the men had a haunting nightmare: in the gloom of the large bunkhouse, his confused cry woke the woman that was sleeping with him. No one knows what his dream was because the next day at four o'clock the *montoneros* were put to rout by Suárez' cavalry* and the pursuit went on for nine leagues, all the way to the now-dusky stubble fields, and the man perished in a ditch, his skull split by a saber from the wars in Peru and Brazil. The woman was named Isidora Cruz; the son she bore was given the name Tadeo Isidoro.

It is not my purpose to repeat the story of his life. Of the days and nights that composed it, I am interested in only one; about the rest, I will recount nothing but that which is essential to an understanding of that single night. The adventure is recorded in a very famous book—that is, in a book whose subject can be all things to all men (I Corinthians 9:22), for it is capable of virtually inexhaustible repetitions, versions, perversions. Those who have commented upon the story of Tadeo Isidoro Cruz, and there are many, stress the influence of the wide plains on his formation, but gauchos just like him were born and died along the forested banks of the Paraná and in the eastern mountain ranges. He did live in a world of monotonous barbarity—when he died in 1874 of the black pox, he had never seen a mountain or a gas jet or a windmill. Or a city: In 1849, he helped drive a herd of stock from Francisco Xavier Acevedo's ranch to Buenos Aires; the drovers went into the city to empty their purses; Cruz, a distrustful sort, never left the inn in the neighborhood of the stockyards. He spent many days there, taciturn, sleeping on the ground, sipping his *mate*, getting up at dawn and lying down again at orisons. He realized (beyond words and even beyond understanding) that the city had nothing to do with him. One of the peons, drunk, made fun of him. Cruz said nothing in reply, but during the nights on the return trip, sitting beside the fire, the other man's mockery continued, so Cruz (who had never shown any anger, or even the slightest resentment) killed him with a single thrust of his knife. Fleeing, he took refuge in a swamp; a few nights later, the cry of a crested screamer warned him that the police had surrounded him. He tested his knife on a leaf. He took off his spurs, so they wouldn't get in his way when the time came—he would fight before he gave himself up. He was wounded in the forearm, the shoulder, and the left hand; he gravely wounded the bravest of the men who'd come to arrest him. When the blood ran down between his fingers, he fought more courageously than ever; toward dawn, made faint by the loss of blood, he was disarmed. Back then, the army served as the country's prison: Cruz was sent to a small fort on the northern frontier. As a low private, he took part in the civil wars; sometimes he fought for his native province, sometimes against it. On January 23, 1856, at the Cardoso Marshes, he was one of the thirty Christian men who, under the command of Sgt. Maj. Eusebio Laprida, battled two hundred Indians.* He was wounded by a spear in that engagement.

There are many gaps in his dark and courageous story. In about

1868, we come across him again on the Pergamino: married or domesticated, the father of a son, the owner of a parcel of land. In 1869 he was made sergeant of the rural police. He had set his past right; at that point in his life, he should have considered himself a happy man, though deep down he wasn't. (In the future, secretly awaiting him, was one lucid, fundamental night—the night when he was finally to see his own face, the night when he was finally to hear his own true name. Once fully understood, that night encompasses his entire story—or rather, one incident, one action on that night does, for actions are the symbol of our selves.) Any life, however long and complicated it may be, actually consists of *a single moment*—the moment when a man knows forever more who he is. It is said that Alexander of Macedonia saw his iron future reflected in the fabulous story of Achilles; Charles XII of Sweden, in the story of Alexander. It was not a book that revealed that knowledge to Tadeo Isidoro Cruz, who did not know how to read; he saw himself in a hand-to-hand cavalry fight and in a man. This is how it happened:

During the last days of June in the year 1870, an order came down for the capture of an outlaw wanted for two murders. The man was a deserter from the forces on the border under the command of Col. Benito Machado; in one drunken spree he had killed a black man in a whorehouse; in another, a resident of the district of Rojas. The report added that he came from Laguna Colorada. It was at Laguna Colorada, forty years earlier, that the *montoneros* had gathered for the catastrophe that had left their flesh for birds and dogs; Laguna Colorado was where Manuel Mesa's career began, before he was executed in the Plaza de la Victoria as the snare drums rolled to drown out the sound of the man's fury*; Laguna Colorada was where the unknown man who fathered Cruz had been born, before he died in a ditch with his skull split by a saber from the battles in Peru and Brazil. Cruz had forgotten the name of the place; with a slight but inexplicable sense of uneasiness he recognized it. . . .On horseback, the outlaw, harried by the soldiers, wove a long labyrinth of turns and switchbacks, but the soldiers finally cornered him on the night of July 12. He had gone to ground in a field of stubble. The darkness was virtually impenetrable; Cruz and his men, cautiously and on foot, advanced toward the brush in whose trembling depths the secret man lurked, or slept. A crested screamer cried; Tadeo Isidoro Cruz had the sense that he had lived the moment before. The outlaw stepped out from his hiding place to fight them. Cruz glimpsed the terrifying apparition—the long mane of hair and the gray beard seemed to consume his face. A well-known reason prevents me from telling the story of that fight; let me simply recall that the deserter gravely wounded or killed several of Cruz' men. As Cruz was fighting in the darkness (as his body was fighting in the darkness), he began to understand. He realized that one destiny is no better than the next and that every man must accept the destiny he bears inside himself. He realized that his sergeant's epaulets and uniform were hampering him. He realized his deep-rooted destiny as a wolf, not a gregarious dog; he realized that the other man was he himself. Day began to dawn on the lawless plain; Cruz threw his cap to the ground, cried that he was not going to be a party to killing a brave man, and he began to fight against the soldiers, alongside the deserter Martín Fierro*

Emma Zunz

On January 14, 1922, when Emma Zunz returned home from the Tarbuch & Loewenthal weaving mill, she found a letter at the far end of the entryway to her building; it had been sent from Brazil, and it informed her that her father had died. She was misled at first by the stamp and the envelope; then the unknown handwriting made her heart flutter. Nine or ten smudgy lines covered almost the entire piece of paper; Emma read that Sr. Maier had accidentally ingested an overdose of veronal and died on the third *inst.* in the hospital at Bagé.* The letter was signed by a resident of the rooming house in which her father had lived, one Fein or Fain, in Rio Grande; he could not have known that he was writing to the dead man's daughter.

Emma dropped the letter. The first thing she felt was a sinking in her stomach and a trembling in her knees; then, a sense of blind guilt, of unreality, of cold, of fear; then, a desire for this day to be past. Then immediately she realized that such a wish was pointless, for her father's death was the only thing that had happened in the world, and it would go on happening, endlessly, forever after. She picked up the piece of paper and went to her room. Furtively, she put it away for safekeeping in a drawer, as though she somehow knew what was coming. She may already have begun to see the things that would happen next; she was already the person she was to become.

In the growing darkness, and until the end of that day, Emma wept over the suicide of Manuel Maier, who in happier days gone by had been Emanuel Zunz. She recalled summer outings to a small farm near Gualeguay,★ she recalled (or tried to recall) her mother, she recalled the family's little house in Lanús★ that had been sold at auction, she recalled the yellow lozenges of a window, recalled the verdict of prison, the disgrace, the anonymous letters with the newspaper article about the "Embezzlement of Funds by Teller," recalled (and this she would never forget) that on the last night, her father had sworn that the thief was Loewenthal— Loewenthal, Aaron Loewenthal, formerly the manager of the mill and now one of its owners. Since 1916, Emma had kept the secret. She had revealed it to no one, not even to Elsa Urstein, her best friend. Perhaps she shrank from it out of profane incredulity; perhaps she thought that the secret was the link between herself and the absent man. Loewenthal didn't know she knew; Emma Zunz gleaned from that minuscule fact a sense of power.

She did not sleep that night, and by the time first light defined the rectangle of the window, she had perfected her plan. She tried to make that day (which seemed interminable to her) be like every other. In the mill, there were rumors of a strike; Emma declared, as she always did, that she was opposed to all forms of violence. At six, when her workday was done, she went with Elsa to a women's club that had a gymnasium and a swimming pool. They joined; she had to repeat and then spell her name; she had to applaud the vulgar jokes that accompanied the struggle to get it correct. She discussed with Elsa and the younger of the Kronfuss girls which moving picture they would see Sunday evening. And then there was talk of boyfriends; no one expected Emma to have anything to say. In April she would be nineteen, but men still inspired in her an almost pathological fear. . . .Home again, she made soup thickened with manioc flakes and some vegetables, ate early, went to bed, and forced herself to sleep. Thus passed Friday the fifteenth—a day of work, bustle, and trivia—the day before *the day*.

On Saturday, impatience wakened her. Impatience, not

nervousness or second thought—and the remarkable sense of relief that she had reached this day at last. There was nothing else for her to plan or picture to herself; within a few hours she would have come to the simplicity of the *fait accompli*. She read in *La Prensa* that the *Nordstjänan*, from Malmö, was to weigh anchor that night from Pier 3; she telephoned Loewenthal, insinuated that she had something to tell him, in confidence, about the strike, and promised to stop by his office at nightfall. Her voice quivered; the quiver befitted a snitch. No other memorable event took place that morning. Emma worked until noon and then settled with Perla Kronfuss and Elsa on the details of their outing on Sunday. She lay down after lunch and with her eyes closed went over the plan she had conceived. She reflected that the final step would be less horrible than the first, and would give her, she had no doubt of it, the taste of victory, and of justice. Suddenly, alarmed, she leaped out of bed and ran to the dressing table drawer. She opened it; under the portrait of Milton Sills, where she had left it night before last, she found Fain's letter. No one could have seen it; she began to read it, and then she tore it up.

To recount with some degree of reality the events of that evening would be difficult, and perhaps inappropriate. One characteristic of hell is its unreality, which might be thought to mitigate hell's terrors but perhaps makes them all the worse. How to make plausible an act in which even she who was to commit it scarcely believed? How to recover those brief hours of chaos that Emma Zunz's memory today repudiates and confuses? Emma lived in Amalgro,* on Calle Liniers*; we know that that evening she went down to the docks. On the infamous Paseo de Julio* she may have seen herself multiplied in mirrors, made public by lights, and stripped naked by hungry eyes—but it is more reasonable to assume that at first she simply wandered, unnoticed, through the indifferent streets. . . .She stepped into two or three bars, observed the routine or the maneuvers of other women. Finally she ran into some men from the *Nordstjärnan*. One of them, who was quite young, she feared might inspire in her some hint of tenderness, so she chose a different one—perhaps a bit shorter than she, and foul-mouthed—so that there might be no mitigation of the purity of the horror. The man led her to a door and then down a gloomy entryway and then to a tortuous stairway and then into a vestibule (with lozenges identical to those of the house in Lanús) and then down a hallway and then to a door that closed behind them. The most solemn of events are outside time— whether because in the most solemn of events the immediate past is severed, as it were, from the future or because the elements that compose those events seem not to be consecutive.

In that time outside time, in that welter of disjointed and horrible sensations, did Emma Zunz think *even once* about the death that inspired the sacrifice? In my view, she thought about it once, and that was enough to endanger her desperate goal. She thought (she could not help thinking) that her father had done to her mother the horrible thing being done to her now. She thought it with weak-limbed astonishment, and then, immediately, took refuge in vertigo. The man—a Swede or Finn—did not speak Spanish; he was an instrument for Emma, as she was for him—but she was used for pleasure, while he was used for justice.

When she was alone, Emma did not open her eyes immediately. On the night table was the money the man had left. Emma sat up and tore it to shreds, as she had torn up the letter a short time before. Tearing up money is an act of impiety, like throwing away bread; the minute she did it, Emma wished she hadn't—an act of pride, and on *that* day. . . .Foreboding melted into the sadness of her body, into the revulsion. Sadness and revulsion lay upon Emma like chains, but slowly she got up and began to dress. The room had no bright colors; the last light of evening made it all the drearier. She managed to slip out without being seen. On the corner she mounted a westbound Lacroze* and following her plan, she sat in the car's frontmost seat, so that no one would see her face. Perhaps she was comforted to see, in the banal bustle of the streets, that what had happened had not polluted everything. She rode through gloomy, shrinking neighborhoods, seeing them and forgetting them instantly, and got off at one of the stops on Warnes.* Paradoxically, her weariness turned into a strength, for it forced her to concentrate on the details of her mission and masked from her its true nature and its final purpose.

Aaron Loewenthal was in the eyes of all an upright man; in those of his few closest acquaintances, a miser. He lived above the mill, alone. Living in the run-down slum, he feared thieves; in the courtyard of the mill there was a big dog, and in his desk drawer, as everyone knew, a revolver. The year before, he had decorously grieved the unexpected death of his wife—a Gauss! who'd brought him an excellent dowry!—but money was his true passion. With secret shame, he knew he was not as good at earning it as at holding on to it. He was quite religious; he believed he had a secret pact with the Lord—in return for prayers and devotions, he was exempted from doing good works. Bald, heavy-set, dressed in mourning, with his dark-lensed pince-nez and blond beard, he was standing next to the window, awaiting the confidential report from operator Zunz.

He saw her push open the gate (which he had left ajar on purpose) and cross the gloomy courtyard. He saw her make a small detour when the dog (tied up on purpose) barked. Emma's lips were moving, like those of a person praying under her breath; weary, over and over they rehearsed the phrases that Sr. Loewenthal would hear before he died.

Things didn't happen the way Emma Zunz had foreseen. Since early the previous morning, many times she had dreamed that she would point the firm revolver, force the miserable wretch to confess his miserable guilt, explain to him the daring stratagem that would allow God's justice to triumph over man's. (It was not out of fear, but because she was an instrument of that justice, that she herself intended not to be punished.) Then, a single bullet in the center of his chest would put an end to Loewenthal's life. But things didn't happen that way.

Sitting before Aaron Loewenthal, Emma felt (more than the urgency to avenge her father) the urgency to punish the outrage she herself had suffered. She could not *not* kill him, after being so fully and thoroughly dishonored. Nor did she have time to waste on theatrics. Sitting timidly in his office, she begged Loewenthal's pardon, invoked (in her guise as snitch) the obligations entailed by loyalty, mentioned a few names, insinuated others, and stopped short, as though overcome by fearfulness. Her performance succeeded; Loewenthal went out to get her a glass of water. By the time he returned from the dining hall, incredulous at the woman's fluttering perturbation yet full of solicitude, Emma had found the heavy revolver in the drawer. She pulled the trigger twice. Loewenthal's considerable body crumpled as though crushed by the explosions and the smoke; the glass of water shattered; his face looked at her with astonishment and fury; the mouth in the face cursed her in Spanish and in Yiddish. The filthy words went on and on; Emma had to shoot him again. Down in the courtyard, the dog, chained to his post, began barking furiously, as a spurt of sudden blood gushed from the obscene lips and sullied the beard and clothes. Emma began the accusation she had prepared ("I have avenged my father, and I shall not be punished . . .") but she didn't finish it, because Sr. Loewenthal was dead. She never knew whether he had managed to understand.

The dog's tyrannical barking reminded her that she couldn't rest, not yet. She mussed up the couch, unbuttoned the dead man's suit coat, removed his spattered pince-nez and left them on the filing-cabinet. Then she picked up the telephone and repeated what she was to repeat so many times, in those and other words: *Something has happened, something unbelievable. . . .Sr. Loewenthal sent for me on the pretext of the strike. . . .He raped me. . . .I killed him. . . .*

The story was unbelievable, yes—and yet it convinced everyone, because in substance it was true. Emma Zunz's tone of voice

49

was real, her shame was real, her hatred was real. The outrage that had been done to her was real, as well; all that was false were the circumstances, the time, and one or two proper names.

The House of Asterion

And the queen gave birth to a son named Asterion.
Apollodorus, *Library, Ill:i*

I know that I am accused of arrogance and perhaps of misanthropy, and perhaps even of madness. These accusations (which I shall punish in due time) are ludicrous. It is true that I never leave my house, but it is also true that its doors (whose number is infinite[1]) stand open night and day to men and also to animals. Anyone who wishes to enter may do so. Here, no womanly splendors, no palatial ostentation shall be found, but only calm and solitude. Here shall be found a house like none other on the face of the earth. (Those who say there is a similar house in Egypt speak lies.) Even my detractors admit that *there is not a single piece of furniture in the house.* Another absurd tale is that I, Asterion, am a prisoner. Need I repeat that the door stands open? Need I add that there is no lock? Furthermore, one afternoon I did go out into the streets; if I returned before nightfall, I did so because of the terrible dread inspired in me by the faces of the people— colorless faces, as flat as the palm of one's hand. The sun had already gone down, but the helpless cry of a babe and the crude supplications of the masses were signs that I had been recognized. The people prayed, fled, fell prostrate before me; some climbed

1. The original reads "fourteen," but there is more than enough cause to conclude that when spoken by Asterion that number stands for "infinite."

up onto the stylobate of the temple of the Axes, others gathered stones. One, I believe, hid in the sea. Not for nothing was my mother a queen; I cannot mix with commoners, even if my modesty should wish it.

The fact is, I am unique. I am not interested in what a man can publish abroad to other men; like the philosopher, I think that nothing can be communicated by the art of writing. Vexatious and trivial minutiæ find no refuge in my spirit, which has been formed for greatness; I have never grasped for long the difference between one letter and another. A certain generous impatience has prevented me from learning to read. Sometimes I regret that, because the nights and the days are long.

Of course I do not lack for distractions. Sometimes I run like a charging ram through the halls of stone until I tumble dizzily to the ground; sometimes I crouch in the shadow of a wellhead or at a corner in one of the corridors and pretend I am being hunted. There are rooftops from which I can hurl myself until I am bloody. I can pretend anytime I like that I am asleep, and lie with my eyes closed and my breathing heavy. (Sometimes I actually fall asleep; sometimes by the time I open my eyes, the color of the day has changed.) But of all the games, the one I like best is pretending that there is another Asterion. I pretend that he has come to visit me, and I show him around the house. Bowing majestically, I say to him: *Now let us return to our previous intersection* or *Let us go this way, now, out into another courtyard* or *I knew that you would like this rain gutter* or *Now you will see a cistern that has filled with sand* or *Now you will see how the cellar forks.* Sometimes I make a mistake and the two of us have a good laugh over it.

It is not just these games I have thought up—I have also thought a great deal about the house. Each part of the house occurs many times; any particular place is another place. There is not one wellhead, one courtyard, one drinking trough, one manger; there are fourteen [an infinite number of] mangers, drinking troughs, courtyards, wellheads. The house is as big as the world—or rather, it *is* the world. Nevertheless, by making my way through every single courtyard with its wellhead and every single dusty gallery of gray stone, I have come out onto the street and seen the temple of the Axes and the sea. That sight, I did not understand until a night vision revealed to me that there are also fourteen [an infinite number of] seas and temples. Everything exists many times, fourteen times, but there are two things in the world that apparently exist but once—on high, the intricate sun, and below, Asterion. Perhaps I have created the stars and the sun and this huge house, and no longer remember it.

Every nine years, nine men come into the house so that I can free them from all evil. I hear their footsteps or their voices far away in the galleries of stone, and I run joyously to find them. The ceremony lasts but a few minutes. One after another, they fall, without my ever having to bloody my hands. Where they fall, they remain, and their bodies help distinguish one gallery from the others. I do not know how many there have been, but I do know that one of them predicted as he died that someday my redeemer would come. Since then, there has been no pain for me in solitude, because I know that my redeemer lives, and in the end he will rise and stand above the dust. If my ear could hear every sound in the world, I would hear his footsteps. I hope he takes me to a place with fewer galleries and fewer doors. What will my redeemer be like, I wonder. Will he be bull or man? Could he possibly be a bull with the face of a man? Or will he be like me?

The morning sun shimmered on the bronze sword. Now there was not a trace of blood left on it.

"Can you believe it, Ariadne?" said Theseus. "The Minotaur scarcely defended itself."

For Maria Mosquera Eastman

The Other Death

About two years ago, I believe it was (I've lost the letter), Gannon wrote me from Gualeguaychú* to announce that he was sending me a translation, perhaps the first to be done into Spanish, of Ralph Waldo Emerson's poem "The Past"; in a postscript he added that Pedro Damián, a man he said he knew I'd remember, had died a few nights earlier of pulmonary congestion. He'd been ravaged by fever, Gannon said, and in his delirium had relived that bloody day at Masoller.* The news struck me as predictable and even trite, because at nineteen or twenty Pedro Damián had followed the banners of Aparicio Saravia.* The 1904 uprising had caught him unawares on a ranch in Río Negro or Paysandu*, where he was working as a common laborer; Damián was from Entre Ríos, Gualeguay* to be exact, but where his friends went, he went—just as spirited and ignorant a fellow as they were. He fought in the occasional hand-to-hand skirmish and in that last battle; repatriated in 1905, he went back (with humble tenacity) to working in the fields. So far as I am aware, he never left his province again. He spent his last thirty years on quite a solitary little farm a league or two from the Ñancay*, it was in that godforsaken place that I spoke with him one evening in 1942—or tried to speak with him. He was a man of few words and little learning. The sound and fury of Masoller were the full extent of his story; it came as no surprise to me that he had relived those times as he lay dying. . . .I had learned that I would never see Damián again, and so I tried to recall him; my visual memory is so bad that all I could remember was a photograph that Gannon had taken of him. That, too, is not particularly remarkable, if you consider that I saw the man himself but once, in early 1942, but saw the photograph countless times. Gannon sent me the photo; I've lost it, but now I've stopped looking for it. I'd be afraid to find it.

The second episode took place in Montevideo, months later. The fever and agonizing death of the man from Entre Ríos suggested to me a tale of fantasy based on the defeat at Masoller; when I told the plot of the story to Emir Rodríguez Monegal, he gave me a letter of introduction to Col. Dionisio Tabares, who had led the campaign. The colonel received me after dinner. From his comfortable rocking chair out in the courtyard, he lovingly and confusedly recalled the old days. He spoke of munitions that never arrived and of exhausted horses, of grimy, sleepy men weaving labyrinths of marches, and of Saravia, who could have entered Montevideo but turned aside "because gauchos have an aversion to the city," of men whose throats were slashed through to the spine,* of a civil war that struck me as more some outlaw's dream than the collision of two armies. He talked about Illescas, Tupambaé, Masoller,* and did so with such perfectly formed periods, and so vividly, that I realized that he'd told these same stories many times before—indeed, it all made me fear that behind his words hardly any memories remained. As he took a breath, I managed to mention the name Damián.

"Damián? Pedro Damián?" the colonel said. "He served with me. A little Indian-like fellow the boys called Daymán." He began a noisy laugh, but suddenly cut it off, with real or pretended discomfort.

It was in another voice that he said that war, like women, served to test a man—before a man goes into battle, he said, no man knows who he truly is. One fellow might think himself a coward and turn out to be a brave man, or it might be the other way around, which was what happened to that poor Damián, who swaggered around the *pulperías* with his white ribbon* and then fell apart in Masoller. There was one shoot-out with the Zumacos* where he'd acted like a man, but it was another thing when the armies squared off and the cannon started in and every man felt like five thousand other men had ganged up to kill 'im. Poor little mestizo bastard, he'd spent his whole life dipping sheep, and all of a sudden he'd gotten himself swept up in that call to defend the nation. . . .

Absurdly, Col. Tabares' version of the events embarrassed me. I'd have preferred that they not have taken place quite that way. Out of the agèd Damián, a man I'd had a glimpse of on a single afternoon, and that, many years ago, I had unwittingly constructed a sort of idol; Tabares' version shattered it. Suddenly I understood Damián's reserve and stubborn solitude; they had been dictated not by modesty, but by shame. Futilely I told myself, over and over, that a man pursued by an act of cowardice is more complex and more interesting than a man who is merely brave. The gaucho Martín Fierro, I thought, is less memorable than Lord Jim or Razumov. Yes, but Damián, as a gaucho, had an obligation to be Martín Fierro—especially so in the company of Uruguayan gauchos. With respect to what Tabares said and failed to say, I caught the gamy taste of what was called *Artiguismo*—the (perhaps unarguable) awareness that Uruguay is more elemental than our own country, and therefore wilder. . . .I recall that that night we said our good-byes with exaggerated effusiveness.

That winter, the lack of one or two details for my tale of fantasy (which stubbornly refused to find its proper shape) made me return to Col. Tabares' house. I found him with another gentleman of a certain age—Dr. Juan Francisco Amaro, of Paysandú, who had also fought in Saravia's uprising. There was talk, predictably enough, of Masoller. Amaro told a few anecdotes and then, slowly, like a man thinking out loud, he added:

"We stopped for the night on the Santa Irene ranch, I remember, and some new men joined up with us. Among them, there was a French veterinarian who died the day before the battle, and a sheep shearer, a young kid from Entre Ríos, named Pedro Damián."

I interrupted sharply—

"I know," I said. "The Argentine kid that fell apart under fire."

I stopped; the two men were looking at me perplexedly.

"I beg your pardon, sir," Amaro said, at last. "Pedro Damián died as any man might wish to die. It was about four in the afternoon. The Red infantry* had dug in on the peak of the hill; our men charged them with lances; Damián led the charge, yelling, and a bullet got him straight in the chest. He stopped stock-still, finished his yell, and crumpled, and his body was trampled under the hooves of the horses. He was dead, and the final charge at Masoller rolled right over him. Such a brave man, and not yet twenty."

He was undoubtedly talking about another Damián, but something made me ask what the young mestizo was yelling.

"Curses," the colonel said, "which is what you yell in charges."

"That may be," said Amaro, "but he was also yelling *¿Viva Urquiza!*"*

We fell silent. Finally, the colonel murmured:

"Not as though he was fighting at Masoller, but at Cagancha or India Muerta,* a hundred years before."

Then, honestly perplexed, he added:

"I commanded those troops, and I'd swear that this is the first time I've heard mention of any Damián."

We could not make him remember.

In Buenos Aires, another incident was to make me feel yet again that shiver that the colonel's forgetfulness had produced in me. Down in the basement of Mitchell's English bookshop, I came upon Patricio Gannon one afternoon, standing before the eleven delectable volumes of the works of Emerson. I asked him how his translation of "The Past" was going. He said he had no plans to translate it; Spanish literature was tedious enough already without Emerson. I reminded him that he had promised me the translation in the same letter in which he'd written me the news of Damián's death. He asked who this "Damián" was. I told him, but drew no response. With the beginnings of a sense of terror I saw that he was looking at me strangely, so I bluffed my way into a literary argument about the sort of person who'd criticize Emerson—a poet more complex, more accomplished, and unquestionably more remarkable, I contended, than poor Edgar Allan Poe.

There are several more events I should record. In April I had a letter from Col. Dionisio Tabares; he was no longer confused—now he remembered quite well the Entre Ríos boy who'd led the charge at Masoller and been buried by his men that night at the foot of the hill. In July I passed through Gualeguaychú; I couldn't manage to find Damián's run-down place—nobody remembered him anymore. I tried to consult the storekeeper, Diego Abaroa, who had seen him die; Abaroa had passed away in the fall. I tried to call to mind Damián's features; months later, as I was browsing through some albums, I realized that the somber face I had managed to call up was the face of the famous tenor Tamberlick, in the role of Otello.

I pass now to hypotheses. The simplest, but also the least satisfactory, posits two Damiáns—the coward who died in Entre Ríos in 1946, and the brave man who died at Masoller in 1904. The problem with that hypothesis is that it doesn't explain the truly enigmatic part of it all: the curious comings and goings of Col. Tabares' memory, the forgetfulness that wipes out the image and even the name of the man that was remembered such a short time ago. (I do not, cannot, accept the even simpler hypothesis—that I might have dreamed the first remembering.) More curious yet is the *supernatural* explanation offered by Ulrike von Kühlmann. Pedro Damián, Ulrike suggests, died in the battle, and at the hour of his death prayed to God to return him to Entre

Ríos. God hesitated a second before granting that favor, and the man who had asked it was already dead, and some men had seen him killed. God, who cannot change the past, although He can change the images of the past, changed the image of death into one of unconsciousness, and the shade of the man from Entre Ríos returned to his native land. Returned, but we should recall that he was a shade, a ghost. He lived in solitude, without wife, without friends; he loved everything, possessed everything, but from a distance, as though from the other side of a pane of glass; he "died," but his gossamer image endured, like water within water. That hypothesis is not correct, but it ought to have suggested the true one (the one that today I *believe* to be the true one), which is both simpler and more outrageous. I discovered it almost magically in Pier Damiani's treatise titled *De omnipotentia*, which I sought out because of two lines from Canto XXI of the *Paradiso*—two lines that deal with a problem of identity. In the fifth chapter of his treatise, Pier Damiani maintains, against Aristotle and Fredegarius of Tours, that God can make what once existed never to have been. I read those old theological arguments and began to understand the tragic story of don Pedro Damián. This is the way I imagine it:

Damián behaved like a coward on the field of Masoller, and he dedicated his life to correcting that shameful moment of weakness. He returned to Entre Ríos; he raised his hand against no man, he "marked" no one,* he sought no reputation for bravery, but in the fields of Ñancay, dealing with the brushy wilderness and the skittish livestock, he hardened himself. Little by little he was preparing himself, unwittingly, for the miracle. Deep inside himself, he thought: If fate brings me another battle, I will know how to deserve it. For forty years he awaited that battle with vague hopefulness, and fate at last brought it to him, at the hour of his death. It brought it in the form of a delirium, but long ago the Greeks knew that we are the shadows of a dream. In his dying agony, he relived his battle, and he acquitted himself like a man—he led the final charge and took a bullet in the chest. Thus, in 1946, by the grace of his long-held passion, Pedro Damián died in the defeat at Masoller, which took place between the winter and spring of the year 1904.

The *Summa Theologica* denies that God can undo, unmake what once existed, but it says nothing about the tangled concatenation of causes and effects—which is so vast and so secret that it is possible that not a *single* remote event can be annulled, no matter how insignificant, without canceling the present. To change the past is not to change a mere single event; it is to annul all its consequences, which tend to infinity. In other words: it is to create two histories of the world. In what we might call the first, Pedro Damián died in Entre Ríos in 1946; in the second, he died at Masoller in 1904. This latter history is the one we are living in now, but the suppression of the former one was not immediate, and it produced the inconsistencies I have reported. In Col. Dionisio Tabares we can see the various stages of this process: at first he remembered that Damián behaved like a coward; then he totally forgot him; then he recalled his impetuous death. The case of the storekeeper Abaroa is no less instructive; he died, in my view, because he had too many memories of don Pedro Damián.

As for myself, I don't think I run a similar risk. I have guessed at and recorded a process inaccessible to humankind, a sort of outrage to rationality; but there are circumstances that mitigate that awesome privilege. For the moment, I am not certain that I have always written the truth. I suspect that within my tale there are false recollections. I suspect that Pedro Damián (if he ever existed) was not called Pedro Damián, and that I remember him under that name in order to be able to believe, someday in the future, that his story was suggested to me by the arguments of Pier Damiani. Much the same thing occurs with that poem that I mentioned in the first paragraph, the poem whose subject is the irrevocability of the past. In 1951 or thereabouts I will recall having concocted a tale of fantasy, but I will have told the story of a true event in much the way that naive Virgil, two thousand years ago, thought he was heralding the birth of a man though he had foretold the birth of God.

Poor Damián! Death carried him off at twenty in a war he knew nothing of and in a homemade sort of battle—yet though it took him a very long time to do so, he did at last achieve his heart's desire, and there is perhaps no greater happiness than that.

Deutsches Requiem

Though he slay me, yet will I trust in him.
Job 13:15

My name is Otto Dietrich zur Linde. One of my forebears, Christoph zur Linde, died in the cavalry charge that decided the victory of Zorndorf. During the last days of 1870, my maternal great-grandfather, Ulrich Forkel, was killed in the Marchenoir forest by French sharpshooters; Captain Dietrich zur Linde, my father, distinguished himself in 1914 at the siege of Namur, and again two years later in the crossing of the Danube.[1] As for myself, I am to be shot as a torturer and a murderer. The court has acted rightly; from the first, I have confessed my guilt. Tomorrow, by the time the prison clock strikes nine, I shall have entered the realms of death; it is natural that I should think of my elders, since I am come so near their shadow—since, somehow, I am they.

During the trial (which fortunately was short) I did not speak; to explain myself at that point would have put obstacles in the way of the verdict and made me appear cowardly. Now things have changed; on this night that precedes my execution, I can speak without fear. I have no desire to be pardoned, for I feel no

---

1. It is significant that zur Linde has omitted his most illustrious forebear, the theologian and Hebraist Johannes Forkel (1799–1846), who applied Hegel's dialectics to Christology and whose literal translation of some of the Apocrypha earned him the censure of Hengstenberg and the praise of Thilo and Gesenius. [Ed.]

guilt, but I do wish to be understood. Those who heed my words shall understand the history of Germany and the future history of the world. I know that cases such as mine, exceptional and shocking now, will very soon be unremarkable. Tomorrow I shall die, but I am a symbol of the generations to come.

I was born in Marienburg in 1908. Two passions, music and metaphysics, now almost forgotten, allowed me to face many terrible years with bravery and even happiness. I cannot list all my benefactors, but there are two names I cannot allow myself to omit: Brahms and Schopenhauer. Frequently, I also repaired to poetry; to those two names, then, I would add another colossal Germanic name: William Shakespeare. Early on, theology had held some interest for me, but I was forever turned from that fantastic discipline (and from Christianity) by Schopenhauer with his direct arguments and Shakespeare and Brahms with the infinite variety of their worlds. I wish anyone who is held in awe and wonder, quivering with tenderness and gratitude, transfixed by some passage in the work of these blessèd men—anyone so touched—to know that I too was once transfixed like them—I the abominable.

Nietzsche and Spengler entered my life in 1927. A certain eighteenth-century author observes that no man wants to owe anything to his contemporaries; in order to free myself from an influence that I sensed to be oppressive, I wrote an article titled *"Abrechnung mit Spengler,"* wherein I pointed out that the most unequivocal monument to those characteristics that the author called Faustian was *not* Goethe's miscellaneous drama[1] but rather a poem written twenty centuries ago, the *De rerum naturæ*. I did,

1. Other nations live naively, in and for themselves, like minerals or meteors; Germany is the universal mirror that receives all others—the conscience of the world (*das Weltbewußtsein*). Goethe is the prototype of that ecumenical mind. I do not criticize him, but I do not see him as the Faustian man of Spengler's treatise.

however, give just due to the sincerity of our philosopher of history, his radically German (*kerndeutsch*) and military spirit. In 1929 I joined the party.

I shall say little about my years of apprenticeship. They were harder for me than for many others, for in spite of the fact that I did not lack valor, I felt no calling for violence. I did, however, realize that we were on the threshold of a new age, and that that new age, like the first years of Islam or Christianity, demanded new men. As individuals, my comrades were odious to me; I strove in vain to convince myself that for the high cause that had brought us all together, we were not individuals.

Theologians claim that if the Lord's attention were to stray for even one second from my right hand, which is now writing, that hand would be plunged into nothingness, as though it had been annihilated by a lightless fire. No one can exist, say I, no one can sip a glass of water or cut off a piece of bread, without justification. That justification is different for every man; I awaited the inexorable war that would test our faith. It was enough for me to know that I would be a soldier in its battles. I once feared that we would be disappointed by the cowardice of England and Russia. Chance (or destiny) wove a different future for me—on March 1, 1939, at nightfall, there were riots in Tilsit, which the newspapers did not report; in the street behind the synagogue, two bullets pierced my leg, and it had to be amputated.[1] Days later, our armies entered Bohemia; when the sirens announced the news, I was in that sedentary hospital, trying to lose myself, forget myself, in the books of Schopenhauer. On the windowsill slept a massive, obese cat—the symbol of my vain destiny.

In the first volume of *Parerga und Paralipomena*, I read once more that all things that can occur to a man, from the moment of his birth to the moment of his death, have been predetermined by him. Thus, all inadvertence is deliberate, every casual encounter

1. It is rumored that the wound had extremely serious consequences. [Ed.]

is an engagement made beforehand, every humiliation is an act of penitence, every failure a mysterious victory, every death a suicide. There is no more cunning consolation than the thought that we have chosen our own misfortunes; that individual theology reveals a secret order, and in a marvelous way confuses ourselves with the deity. What unknown purpose (I thought) had made me seek out that evening, those bullets, this mutilation? Not the fear of war—I knew that; something deeper. At last I believed I understood. To die for a religion is simpler than living that religion fully; battling savage beasts in Ephesus is less difficult (thousands of obscure martyrs did it) than being Paul, the servant of Jesus Christ; a single act is quicker than all the hours of a man. The battle and the glory are *easy*; Raskolnikov's undertaking was more difficult than Napoleon's. On February 7, 1941, I was made subdirector of the Tarnowitz concentration camp.

Carrying out the duties attendant on that position was not something I enjoyed, but I never sinned by omission. The coward proves himself among swords; the merciful man, the compassionate man, seeks to be tested by jails and others' pain. Nazism is intrinsically a *moral* act, a stripping away of the old man, which is corrupt and depraved, in order to put on the new. In battle, amid the captains' outcries and the shouting, such a transformation is common; it is not common in a crude dungeon, where insidious compassion tempts us with ancient acts of tenderness. I do not write that word "compassion" lightly: compassion on the part of the superior man is Zarathustra's ultimate sin. I myself (I confess) almost committed it when the famous poet David Jerusalem was sent to us from Breslau.

Jerusalem was a man of fifty; poor in the things of this world, persecuted, denied, calumniated, he had consecrated his genius to hymns of happiness. I think I recall that in the *Dichtung der Zeit*, Albert Sörgel compared him to Whitman. It is not a happy comparison: Whitman celebrates the universe *a priori*, in a way that is general and virtually indifferent; Jerusalem takes delight in every smallest thing, with meticulous and painstaking love. He never stoops to enumerations, catalogs. I can still recite many hexameters from that profound poem titled "Tse Yang, Painter of Tigers," which is virtually striped with tigers, piled high with transversal, silent tigers, riddled through and through with tigers. Nor shall I ever forget the soliloquy "Rosenkranz Talks with the Angel," in which a sixteenth-century London moneylender tries in vain, as he is dying, to exculpate himself, never suspecting that the secret justification for his life is that he has inspired one of his clients (who has seen him only once, and has no memory even of that) to create the character Shylock. A man of memorable eyes, sallow skin, and a beard that was almost black, David Jerusalem was the prototypical Sephardic Jew, although he belonged to the depraved and hated Ashkenazim. I was severe with him; I let neither compassion nor his fame make me soft. I had realized many years before I met David Jerusalem that everything in the world can be the seed of a possible hell; a face, a word, a compass, an advertisement for cigarettes—anything can drive a person insane if that person cannot manage to put it out of his mind. Wouldn't a man be mad if he constantly had before his mind's eye the map of Hungary? I decided to apply this principle to the disciplinary regimen of our house, and . . .[1] In late 1942, Jerusalem went insane; on March 1, 1943, he succeeded in killing himself.[2]

I do not know whether Jerusalem understood that if I destroyed him, it was in order to destroy my own compassion. In my eyes, he was not a man, not even a Jew; he had become a symbol of a

1. Here, the excision of a number of lines has been unavoidable. [Ed.]
2. In neither the files nor the published work of Sörgel does Jerusalem's name appear. Nor does one find it in the histories of German literature. I do not, however, think that this is an invented figure. Many Jewish intellectuals were tortured in Tarnowitz on the orders of Otto Dietrich zur Linde, among them the pianist Emma Rosenzweig. "David Jerusalem" is perhaps a symbol for many individuals. We are told that he died on March 1, 1943; on March 1, 1939, the narrator had been wounded at Tilsit. [Ed.]

detested region of my soul. I suffered with him, I died with him, I somehow have been lost with him; that was why I was implacable.

Meanwhile, the grand days and grand nights of a thrilling war washed over us. In the air we breathed there was an emotion that resembled love. As though the ocean were suddenly nearby, there was a tonic and an exultation in the blood. In those years, everything was different—even the taste of one's sleep. (I may never have been happy, but it is common knowledge that misery requires paradises lost.) There is no man who does not long for plenitude—the sum of the experiences of which a man is capable; there is no man who does not fear being defrauded of a part of that infinite inheritance. But my generation has had it all, for first it was given glory, and then defeat.

In October or November of 1942, my brother Friedrich died in the second Battle of El Alamein, on the Egyptian sands; months later, an aerial bombardment destroyed the house we had been born in; another, in late 1943, destroyed my laboratory. Hounded across vast continents, the Third Reich was dying; its hand was against all men, and all men's hands against it. Then, something remarkable happened, and now I think I understand it. I believed myself capable of drinking dry the cup of wrath, but when I came to the dregs I was stopped by an unexpected flavor—the mysterious and almost horrific taste of happiness. I tested several explanations; none satisfied me. *I feel a contentment in defeat*, I reflected, *because secretly I know my own guilt, and only punishment can redeem me.* Then *I feel a contentment in defeat*, I reflected, *simply because defeat has come, because it is infinitely connected to all the acts that are, that were, and that shall be, because to censure or deplore a single real act is to blaspheme against the universe.* I tested those arguments, as I say, and at last I came to the true one.

It has been said that all men are born either Aristotelians or Platonists. That is equivalent to saying that there is no debate of an abstract nature that is not an instance of the debate between

Aristotle and Plato. Down through the centuries and latitudes, the names change, the dialects, the faces, but not the eternal antagonists. Likewise, the history of nations records a secret continuity. When Arminius slaughtered the legions of Varus in a swamp, when he slashed their throats, he did not know that he was a forerunner of a German Empire; Luther, the translator of the Bible, never suspected that his destiny would be to forge a nation that would destroy the Bible forever; Christoph zur Linde, killed by a Muscovite bullet in 1758, somehow set the stage for the victories of 1914; Hitler thought he was fighting for *a* nation, but he was fighting for *all* nations, even for those he attacked and abominated. It does not matter that his *ego* was unaware of that; his blood, his *will*, knew. The world was dying of Judaism, and of that disease of Judaism that is belief in Christ; we proffered it violence and faith in the sword. That sword killed us, and we are like the wizard who weaves a labyrinth and is forced to wander through it till the end of his days, or like David, who sits in judgment on a stranger and sentences him to death, and then hears the revelation: *Thou art that man.* There are many things that must be destroyed in order to build the new order; now we know that Germany was one of them. We have given something more than our lives; we have given the life of our belovèd nation. Let others curse and others weep; I rejoice in the fact that our gift is orbicular and perfect.

Now an implacable age looms over the world. We forged that age, we who are now its victim. What does it matter that England is the hammer and we the anvil? What matters is that violence, not servile Christian acts of timidity, now rules. If victory and injustice and happiness do not belong to Germany, let them belong to other nations. Let heaven exist, though our place be in hell.

I look at my face in the mirror in order to know who I am, in order to know how I shall comport myself within a few hours, when I face the end. My flesh may feel fear; I *myself* do not.

Averroës' Search

S'imaginant que la tragédie n'est autre chose que l'art
de louer. . . .   Ernest Renan, *Averroès, 48 (1861)*

Abu-al-Walīd Muhammad ibn-Ahmad ibn-Rushd (it would take
that long name, passing through "Benraist" and "Avenris" and
even "Aben Rassad" and "Filius Rosadis," a hundred years to
become "Averroës") was at work on the eleventh chapter of his
work *Tahāfut al-Tahāfut* ("Destruction of the Destruction"), which
maintains, contrary to the Persian ascetic al-Ghazzāli, author of
the *Tahāfut al-Falāsifah* ("Destruction of Philosophers"), that the
deity knows only the general laws of the universe, those that
apply not to the individual but to the species. He wrote with slow
assurance, from right to left; the shaping of syllogisms and linking
together of vast paragraphs did not keep him from feeling, like a
sense of wonderful well-being, the cool, deep house around him.
In the depths of the siesta, loving turtledoves purred throatily,
one to another; from some invisible courtyard came the murmur
of a fountain; something in the flesh of Averroës, whose ancestors
had come from the deserts of Arabia, was grateful for the steadfast
presence of the water. Below lay the gardens of flowers and of
foodstuffs; below that ran the bustling Guadalquivir; beyond the
river spread the beloved city of Córdoba, as bright as Baghdad
or Cairo, like a complex and delicate instrument; and, encircling
Córdoba (this, Averroës could feel too), extending to the very
frontier, stretched the land of Spain, where there were not a great

69

many things, yet where each thing seemed to exist materially and eternally.

His quill ran across the page, the arguments, irrefutable, knitted together, and yet a small worry clouded Averroës' happiness. Not the sort of worry brought on by the *Tahāfut*, which was a fortuitous enterprise, but rather a philological problem connected with the monumental work that would justify him to all people—his commentary on Aristotle. That Greek sage, the fountainhead of all philosophy, had been sent down to men to teach them all things that can be known; interpreting Aristotle's works, in the same way the *ulemas* interpret the Qur'ān, was the hard task that Averroës had set himself. History will record few things lovelier and more moving than this Arab physician's devotion to the thoughts of a man separated from him by a gulf of fourteen centuries. To the intrinsic difficulties of the enterprise we might add that Averroës, who knew neither Syriac nor Greek, was working from a translation of a translation. The night before, two doubtful words had halted him at the very portals of the Poetics. Those words were "tragedy" and "comedy." He had come across them years earlier, in the third book of the Rhetoric; no one in all of Islam could hazard a guess as to their meaning. He had pored through the pages of Alexander of Aphrodisias, compared the translations of the Nestorian Hunayn ibn-Ishāq and Abu-Bashār Māta—and he had found nothing. Yet the two arcane words were everywhere in the text of the Poetics—it was impossible to avoid them.

Averroës laid down his quill. He told himself (without conviction) that what we seek is often near at hand, put away the manuscript of the *Tahāfut*, and went to the shelf on which the many volumes of blind ibn-Sīna's *Moqqām*, copied by Persian copyists, stood neatly aligned. Of course he had already consulted them, but he was tempted by the idle pleasure of turning their pages. He was distracted from that scholarly distraction by a kind of song. He looked out through the bars of the balcony; there below, in the narrow earthen courtyard, half-naked children were at play. One of them, standing on the shoulders of another, was clearly playing at being a muezzin: his eyes tightly closed, he was chanting the muezzin's monotonous cry, *There is no God but Allah.* The boy standing motionless and holding him on his shoulders was the turret from which he sang; another, kneeling, bowing low in the dirt, was the congregation of the faithful. The game did not last long—they all wanted to be the muezzin, no one wanted to be the worshippers or the minaret. Averroës listened to them arguing in the "vulgar" dialect (that is, the incipient Spanish) of the Muslim masses of the Peninsula. He opened Khalil's *Kitāb al-'Ayn* and thought proudly that in all of Córdoba (perhaps in all of Al-Andalus) there was no other copy of the perfect work—only this one, sent him by Emir Ya'qūb al-Mansūr from Tangier. The name of that port reminded him that the traveler abu-al-Hasan al-Ash'ari, who had returned from Morocco, was to dine with him that evening at the home of the Qur'ānist Faraj. Abu-al-Hasan claimed to have reached the kingdoms of the Sin Empire [China]; with that peculiar logic born of hatred, his detractors swore that he had never set foot in China and that he had blasphemed Allah in the temples of that land. The gathering would inevitably last for hours; Averroës hurriedly went back to his work on the *Tahāfut.* He worked until dusk.

At Faraj's house, the conversation moved from the incomparable virtues of the governor to those of his brother the emir; then, out in the garden, the talk was of roses. Abu-al-Hasan (having never seen them) said there were no roses like those which bedeck the villas of Andalusia. Faraj was not to be suborned by flattery; he observed that the learnèd ibn-Qutaybah had described a superb variety of *perpetual* rose which grows in the gardens of Hindustan and whose petals, of a deep crimson red, exhibit characters reading *There is no God but Allah, and Muhammad is His prophet.* He added that abu-al-Hasan must surely be acquainted with those roses. Abu-al-Hasan looked at him in alarm. If he said yes, he would be judged by all, quite rightly, to be the most pliable and serviceable of impostors; if he said no, he would be judged an infidel. He opted to breathe that Allah held the keys that unlock hidden things, and that there was no green or wilted thing on earth that was not recorded in His Book. Those words belong to one of the first sūras of the Qur'ān; they were received with a reverential murmur. Puffed up by that victory of dialectics, abu-al-Hasan was about to declare that Allah is perfect in His works, and inscrutable. But Averroës, prefiguring the distant arguments of a still-problematic Hume, interrupted.

"I find it less difficult to accept an error in the learnèd ibn-Qutaybah, or in the copyists," he said, "than to accept that the earth brings forth roses with the profession of our faith."

"Precisely. Great words and true," said abu-al-Hasan.

"Some traveler, I recall," mused the poet Abd-al-Malik, "speaks of a tree whose branches put forth green birds. I am pained less by believing in that tree than in roses adorned with letters."

"The birds' color," said Averroës, "does seem to make that wonder easier to bear. In addition, both birds and the fruit of trees belong to the natural world, while writing is an art. To move from leaves to birds is easier than to move from roses to letters."

Another guest indignantly denied that writing was an art, since the original Book of the Qur'ān—*the mother of the Book*—predates the Creation, and resides in heaven. Another spoke of Al-Jāhiz of Basra, who had stated that the Qur'ān is a substance that can take the form of man or animal—an opinion which appears to agree with that of the people who attribute to the Qur'ān two faces. Faraj discoursed long on orthodox doctrine. The Qur'ān, he said, is one of the attributes of Allah, even as His Mercy is; it may be copied in a book, pronounced with the tongue, or remembered in the heart, but while language and signs and writing are the work of men, the Qur'ān itself is irrevocable and eternal. Averroës, who had written his commentary on the *Republic*, might have said that the mother of the Book is similar, in a way, to the Platonic Idea, but he could see that theology was one subject utterly beyond the grasp of abu-al-Hasan.

Others, who had come to the same realization, urged abu-al-Hasan to tell a tale of wonder. Then, like now, the world was horrible; daring men might wander through it, but so might wretches, those who fall down in the dust before all things. Abu-al-Hasan's memory was a mirror of secret acts of cowardice. What story could he tell? Besides, the guests demanded marvels, while the marvelous was perhaps incommunicable: the moon of Bengal is not the same as the moon of Yemen, but it deigns to be described with the same words. Abu-al-Hasan pondered; then, he spoke:

"He who wanders through climes and cities," his unctuous voice began, "sees many things worthy of belief. This, for instance, which I have told but once before, to the king of the Turks. It took place in Sin-i Kalal [Canton], where the River of the Water of Life spills into the sea."

Faraj asked whether the city lay many leagues from that wall erected by Iskandar dhu-al-Quarnayn [Alexander of Macedonia] to halt the advance of Gog and Magog.

"There are vast deserts between them," abu-al-Hasan said, with inadvertent haughtiness. "Forty days must a *kafila* [caravan] travel before catching sight of its towers, and another forty, men say, before the *kafila* stands before them. In Sin-i Kalal I know of no man who has seen it or seen the man who has seen it."

For one moment the fear of the grossly infinite, of mere space, mere matter, laid its hand on Averroës. He looked at the symmetrical garden; he realized that he was old, useless, unreal. Then abu-al-Hasan spoke again:

"One evening, the Muslim merchants of Sin-i Kalal conducted me to a house of painted wood in which many persons lived. It is not possible to describe that house, which was more like a single room, with rows of cabinet-like contrivances, or balconies,

73

one atop another. In these niches there were people eating and drinking; there were people sitting on the floor as well, and also on a raised terrace. The people on this terrace were playing the tambour and the lute—all, that is, save some fifteen or twenty who wore crimson masks and prayed and sang and conversed among themselves. These masked ones suffered imprisonment, but no one could see the jail; they rode upon horses, but the horse was not to be seen; they waged battle, but the swords were of bamboo; they died, and then they walked again."

"The acts of madmen," said Faraj, "are beyond that which a sane man can envision."

"They were not madmen," abu-al-Hasan had to explain. "They were, a merchant told me, presenting a story."

No one understood, no one seemed to want to understand. Abu-al-Hasan, in some confusion, swerved from the tale he had been telling them into inept explanation. Aiding himself with his hands, he said:

"Let us imagine that someone *shows* a story instead of telling it—the story of the seven sleepers of Ephesus, say.* We see them retire into the cavern, we see them pray and sleep, we see them sleep with their eyes open, we see them grow while they are asleep, we see them awaken after three hundred nine years, we see them hand the merchant an ancient coin, we see them awaken in paradise, we see them awaken with the dog. It was something like that that the persons on the terrace showed us that evening."

"Did these persons speak?" asked Faraj.

"Of course they did," said abu-al-Hasan, now become the apologist for a performance that he only barely recalled and that had irritated him considerably at the time. "They spoke and sang and gave long boring speeches!"

"In that case," said Faraj, "there was no need for *twenty* persons. A single speaker could *tell* anything, no matter how complex it might be."

To that verdict, they all gave their nod. They extolled the

virtues of Arabic—the language used by Allah, they recalled, when He instructs the angels—and then the poetry of the Arabs. After according that poetry its due praise, abu-al-Hasan dismissed those other poets who, writing in Còrdoba or Damascus, clung to pastoral images and Bedouin vocabulary—outmoded, he called them. He said it was absurd for a man whose eyes beheld the wide Guadalquivir to compose odes upon the water of a well. It was time, he argued, that the old metaphors be renewed; back when Zuhayr compared fate to a blind camel, he said, the figure was arresting—but five hundred years of admiration had worn it very thin. To that verdict, which they had all heard many times before, from many mouths, they all likewise gave their nod. Averroës, however, kept silent. At last he spoke, not so much to the others as to himself.

"Less eloquently," he said, "and yet with similar arguments, I myself have sometimes defended the proposition argued now by abu-al-Hasan. In Alexandria there is a saying that only the man who has already committed a crime and repented of it is incapable of that crime; to be free of an erroneous opinion, I myself might add, one must at some time have professed it. In his *mu'allaqa*, Zuhayr says that in the course of his eighty years of pain and glory many is the time he has seen destiny trample men, like an old blind camel; abu-al-Hasan says that that figure no longer makes us marvel. One might reply to that objection in many ways. First, that if the purpose of the poem were to astound, its life would be not measured in centuries but in days, or hours, or perhaps even minutes. Second, that a famous poet is less an inventor than a discoverer. In praise of ibn-Sharaf of Berkha, it has many times been said that only he was capable of imagining that the stars of the morning sky fall gently, like leaves falling from the trees; if that were true, it would prove only that the image is trivial. The image that only a single man can shape is an image that interests no man. There are infinite things upon the earth; any one of them can be compared to any other. Comparing

75

stars to leaves is no less arbitrary than comparing them to fish, or birds. On the other hand, every man has surely felt at some moment in his life that destiny is powerful yet clumsy, innocent yet inhuman. It was in order to record that feeling, which may be fleeting or constant but which no man may escape experiencing, that Zuhayr's line was written. No one will ever say better what Zuhayr said there. Furthermore (and this is perhaps the essential point of my reflections), time, which ravages fortresses and great cities, only *enriches* poetry. At the time it was composed by him in Arabia, Zuhayr's poetry served to bring together two images—that of the old camel and that of destiny; repeated today, it serves to recall Zuhayr and to conflate our own tribulations with those of that dead Arab. The figure *had* two terms; today, it *has* four. Time widens the circle of the verses, and I myself know some verses that are, like music, all things to all men. Thus it was that many years ago, in Marrakesh, tortured by memories of Córdoba, I soothed myself by repeating the apostrophe which 'Abd-al-Rahmān spoke in the gardens of al-Rusayfah to an African palm:

> *Thou too art, oh palm!,*
> *On this foreign soil . . .*

"A remarkable gift, the gift bestowed by poetry—words written by a king homesick for the Orient served to comfort me when I was far away in Africa, homesick for Spain."

Then Averroës spoke of the first poets, those who in the Time of Ignorance, before Islam, had already said all things in the infinite language of the deserts. Alarmed (and not without reason) by the inane versifications of ibn-Sharaf, he said that in the ancients and the Qur'ān could all poetry be read, and he condemned as illiterate and vain all desire to innovate. The others listened with pleasure, for he was vindicating that which was old.

Muezzins were calling the faithful to the prayer of first light when Averroës entered his library again. (In the harem, the black-haired slave girls had tortured a red-haired slave girl, but Averroës was not to know that until evening.) Something had revealed to him the meaning of the two obscure words. With firm, painstaking calligraphy, he added these lines to the manuscript: *Aristu* [Aristotle] *gives the name "tragedy" to panegyrics and the name "comedy" to satires and anathemas. There are many admirable tragedies and comedies in the Qur'ān and the* mu'allaqat *of the mosque.*

He felt sleep coming upon him, he felt a chill. His turban unwound, he looked at himself in a metal mirror. I do not know what his eyes beheld, for no historian has described the forms of his face. I know that he suddenly disappeared, as though annihilated by a fire without light, and that with him disappeared the house and the unseen fountain and the books and the manuscripts and the turtledoves and the many black-haired slave girls and the trembling red-haired slave girl and Faraj and abu-al-Hasan and the rosebushes and perhaps even the Guadalquivir.

In the preceding tale, I have tried to narrate the process of failure, the process of defeat. I thought first of that archbishop of Canterbury who set himself the task of proving that God exists; then I thought of the alchemists who sought the philosopher's stone; then, of the vain trisectors of the angle and squarers of the circle. Then I reflected that a more poetic case than these would be a man who sets himself a goal that is not forbidden to other men, but is forbidden to him. I recalled Averroës, who, bounded within the circle of Islam, could never know the meaning of the words *tragedy* and *comedy*. I told his story; as I went on, I felt what that god mentioned by Burton must have felt—the god who set himself the task of creating a bull but turned out a buffalo. I felt that the work mocked me, foiled me, thwarted me. I felt that Averroës, trying to imagine what a play is without ever having suspected what a theater is, was no more absurd than I, trying to imagine Averroës yet with no more material than a few snatches from Renan, Lane, and Asín Palacios. I felt, on the last page, that my story was a symbol of the man I had been as I was writing it, and that in order to write that story I had had to be that man, and that in order to be that man I had had to write that story, and so on, *ad infinitum*. (And just when I stop believing in him, "Averroës" disappears.)

The Zahir

In Buenos Aires the Zahir is a common twenty-centavo coin into which a razor or letter opener has scratched the letters *N T* and the number 2; the date stamped on the face is 1929. (In Gujarat, at the end of the eighteenth century, the Zahir was a tiger; in Java it was a blind man in the Surakarta mosque, stoned by the faithful; in Persia, an astrolabe that Nadir Shah ordered thrown into the sea; in the prisons of Mahdi, in 1892, a small sailor's compass, wrapped in a shred of cloth from a turban, that Rudolf Karl von Slatin touched; in the synagogue in Córdoba, according to Zotenberg, a vein in the marble of one of the twelve hundred pillars; in the ghetto in Tetuán, the bottom of a well.) Today is the thirteenth of November; last June 7, at dawn, the Zahir came into my hands; I am not the man I was then, but I am still able to recall, and perhaps recount, what happened. I am still, albeit only partially, Borges.

On June 6, Teodelina Villar died. Back in 1930, photographs of her had littered the pages of worldly magazines; that ubiquity may have had something to do with the fact that she was thought to be a very pretty woman, although that supposition was not unconditionally supported by every image of her. But no matter—Teodelina Villar was less concerned with beauty than with perfection. The Jews and Chinese codified every human situation: the *Mishnah* tells us that beginning at sunset on the Sabbath, a tailor may not go into the street carrying a needle; the Book of Rites informs us that a guest receiving his first glass of wine must assume a grave demeanor; receiving the second, a respectful, happy air. The discipline that Teodelina Villar imposed upon herself was analogous, though even more painstaking and detailed. Like Talmudists and Confucians, she sought to make every action irreproachably correct, but her task was even more admirable and difficult than theirs, for the laws of her creed were not eternal, but sensitive to the whims of Paris and Hollywood. Teodelina Villar would make her entrances into orthodox places, at the orthodox hour, with orthodox adornments, and with ortho-dox world-weariness, but the world-weariness, the adornments, the hour, and the places would almost immediately pass out of fashion, and so come to serve (upon the lips of Teodelina Villar) for the very epitome of "tackiness." She sought the absolute, like Flaubert, but the absolute in the ephemeral. Her life was exemplary, and yet an inner desperation constantly gnawed at her. She passed through endless metamorphoses, as though fleeing from herself; her coiffure and the color of her hair were famously unstable, as were her smile, her skin, and the slant of her eyes. From 1932 on, she was studiedly thin. . . .The war gave her a great deal to think about. With Paris occupied by the Germans, how was one to follow fashion? A foreign man she had always had her doubts about was allowed to take advantage of her good will by selling her a number of stovepipe-shaped *chapeaux*. Within a year, it was revealed that those ridiculous shapes *had never been worn in Paris*, and therefore were not *hats*, but arbitrary and unauthorized *caprices*. And it never rains but it pours: Dr. Villar had to move to Calle Aráoz* and his daughter's image began to grace advertisements for face creams and automobiles—face creams she never used and automobiles she could no longer afford! Teodelina knew that the proper exercise of her art required a great fortune; she opted to retreat rather than surrender. And besides—it pained her to compete with mere insubstantial *girls*. The sinister apartment on Aráoz, however, was too much to bear; on June 6, Teodelina Villar committed the breach of decorum of dying in the middle of Barrio Sur. Shall I confess that moved by the sincerest of Argentine passions—snobbery—I was in love with her, and that her death actually brought tears to my eyes? Perhaps the reader had already suspected that.

At wakes, the progress of corruption allows the dead person's body to recover its former faces. At some point on the confused night of June 6, Teodelina Villar magically became what she had been twenty years before; her features recovered the authority that arrogance, money, youth, the awareness of being the *crème de la crème*, restrictions, a lack of imagination, and stolidity can give. My thoughts were more or less these: No version of that face that had so disturbed me shall ever be as memorable as this one; really, since it could almost be the first, it ought to be the last. I left her lying stiff among the flowers, her contempt for the world growing every moment more perfect in death. It was about two o'clock, I would guess, when I stepped into the street. Outside, the predictable ranks of one- and two-story houses had taken on that abstract air they often have at night, when they are simplified by darkness and silence. Drunk with an almost impersonal pity, I wandered through the streets. On the corner of Chile and Tacuarí* I spotted an open bar-and-general-store. In that establishment, to my misfortune, three men were playing *truco*.*

In the rhetorical figure known as *oxymoron*, the adjective applied to a noun seems to contradict that noun. Thus, gnostics spoke of a "dark light" and alchemists, of a "black sun." Departing from my last visit to Teodelina Villar and drinking a glass of harsh brandy in a corner bar-and-grocery-store was a kind of oxymoron: the very vulgarity and facileness of it were what tempted me. (The fact that men were playing cards in the place increased the contrast.) I asked the owner for a brandy and orange juice; among my change I was given the Zahir; I looked at it for an instant, then walked outside into the street, perhaps with the beginnings of a fever. The thought struck me that there is no coin that is not the symbol of all the coins that shine endlessly down throughout history and fable. I thought of Charon's obolus; the alms that Belisarius went about begging for; Judas' thirty pieces of silver; the drachmas of the courtesan Laïs; the ancient coin proffered by one of the Ephesian sleepers; the bright coins of the wizard in the *1001 Nights*, which turned into disks of paper; Isaac Laquedem's inexhaustible denarius; the sixty thousand coins, one for every line of an epic, which Firdusi returned to a king because they were silver and not gold; the gold doubloon nailed by Ahab to the mast; Leopold Bloom's unreturning florin; the gold louis that betrayed the fleeing Louis XVI near Varennes. As though in a dream, the thought that in any coin one may read those famous connotations seemed to me of vast, inexplicable importance. I wandered, with increasingly rapid steps, through the deserted streets and plazas. Weariness halted me at a corner. My eyes came to rest on a woebegone wrought-iron fence; behind it, I saw the black-and-white tiles of the porch of La Concepción.* I had wandered in a circle; I was just one block from the corner where I'd been given the Zahir.

I turned the corner; the chamfered curb in darkness* at the far end of the street showed me that the establishment had closed. On Belgrano I took a cab. Possessed, without a trace of sleepiness, almost happy, I reflected that there is nothing less material than money, since any coin (a twenty-centavo piece, for instance) is, in all truth, a panoply of possible futures. *Money is abstract*, I said over and over, *money is future time.* It can be an evening just outside the city, or a Brahms melody, or maps, or chess, or coffee, or the words of Epictetus, which teach contempt of gold; it is a Proteus more changeable than the Proteus of the isle of Pharos. It is unforeseeable time, Bergsonian time, not the hard, solid time of Islam or the Porch. Adherents of determinism deny that there is any event in the world that is *possible*, i.e., that *might* occur; a coin symbolizes our free will. (I had no suspicion at the time that these "thoughts" were an artifice against the Zahir and a first manifestation of its demonic influence.) After long and pertinacious musings, I at last fell asleep, but I dreamed that I was a pile of coins guarded by a gryphon.

The next day I decided I'd been drunk. I also decided to free myself of the coin that was affecting me so distressingly. I looked at it—there was nothing particularly distinctive about it, except those scratches. Burying it in the garden or hiding it in a corner of the library would have been the best thing to do, but I wanted to escape its orbit altogether, and so preferred to "lose" it. I went neither to the Basílica del Pilar that morning nor to the cemetery*; I took a subway to Constitución and from Constitución to San Juan and Boedo. On an impulse, I got off at Urquiza; I walked toward the west and south; I turned left and right, with studied randomness, at several corners, and on a street that looked to me like all the others I went into the first tavern I came to, ordered a brandy, and paid with the Zahir. I half closed my eyes, even behind the dark lenses of my spectacles, and managed not to see the numbers on the houses or the name of the street. That night, I took a sleeping draft and slept soundly.

Until the end of June I distracted myself by composing a tale of fantasy. The tale contains two or three enigmatic circumlocutions—*sword-water* instead of *blood*, for example, and *dragon's-bed* for *gold*—and is written in the first person. The narrator is an ascetic who has renounced all commerce with mankind and lives on a kind of moor. (The name of the place is Gnitaheidr.) Because of the simplicity and innocence of his life, he is judged by some to be an angel; that is a charitable sort of exaggeration, because no one is free of sin—he himself (to take the example nearest at hand) has cut his father's throat, though it is true that his father was a famous wizard who had used his magic to usurp an infinite treasure to himself. Protecting this treasure from cankerous human greed is the mission to which the narrator has devoted his life; day and night he stands guard over it. Soon, perhaps too soon, that watchfulness will come to an end: the stars have told him that the sword that will sever it forever has already been forged. (The name of the sword is Gram.) In an increasingly tortured style, the narrator praises the lustrousness and flexibility of his body; one paragraph offhandedly mentions "scales"; another says that the treasure he watches over is of red rings and gleaming gold. At the end, we realize that the ascetic is the serpent Fafnir and the treasure on which the creature lies coiled is the gold of the Nibelungen. The appearance of Sigurd abruptly ends the story.

I have said that composing that piece of trivial nonsense (in the course of which I interpolated, with pseudoerudition, a line or two from the *Fafnismal*) enabled me to put the coin out of my mind. There were nights when I was so certain I'd be able to forget it that I would willfully remember it. The truth is, I abused those moments; starting to recall turned out to be much easier than stopping. It was futile to tell myself that that abominable nickel disk was no different from the infinite other identical, inoffensive disks that pass from hand to hand every day. Moved by that reflection, I attempted to think about another coin, but I couldn't. I also recall another (frustrated) experiment that I performed with Chilean five- and ten-centavo pieces and a Uruguayan two-centavo piece. On July 16, I acquired a pound sterling; I didn't look at it all that day, but that night (and others) I placed it under a magnifying glass and studied it in the light of a powerful electric lamp. Then I made a rubbing of it. The rays of light and the dragon and St. George availed me naught; I could not rid myself of my *idée fixe*.

In August, I decided to consult a psychiatrist. I did not confide the entire absurd story to him; I told him I was tormented by insomnia and that often I could not free my mind of the image of an object, any random object—a coin, say. . . .A short time later, in a bookshop on Calle Sarmiento, I exhumed a copy of Julius Barlach's *Urkunden zur Geschichte der Zahirsage* (Breslau, 1899).

Between the covers of that book was a description of my illness. The introduction said that the author proposed to "gather into a single manageable octavo volume every existing document that bears upon the superstition of the Zahir, including four articles held in the Habicht archives and the original manuscript of Philip Meadows Taylor's report on the subject." Belief in the Zahir is of Islamic ancestry, and dates, apparently, to sometime in the eighteenth century. (Barlach impugns the passages that Zotenberg attributes to Abul-Feddah.) In Arabic, "*zahir*" means visible, manifest, evident; in that sense, it is one of the ninety-nine names of God; in Muslim countries, the masses use the word for "beings or things which have the terrible power to be unforgettable, and whose image eventually drives people mad." Its first undisputed witness was the Persian polymath and dervish Lutf Ali Azur; in the corroborative pages of the biographical encyclopedia titled *Temple of Fire*, Ali Azur relates that in a certain school in Shiraz there was a copper astrolabe "constructed in such a way that any man that looked upon it but once could think of nothing else, so that the king commanded that it be thrown into the deepest depths of the sea, in order that men might not forget the universe." Meadows Taylor's account is somewhat more extensive; the author served the Nazim of Hyderabad and composed the famous novel *Confessions of a Thug*. In 1832, on the outskirts of Bhuj, Taylor heard the following uncommon expression used to signify madness or saintliness: "Verily he has looked upon the tiger." He was told that the reference was to a magic tiger that was the perdition of all who saw it, even from a great distance, for never afterward could a person stop thinking about it. Someone mentioned that one of those stricken people had fled to Mysore, where he had painted the image of the tiger in a palace. Years later, Taylor visited the prisons of that district; in the jail at Nighur, the governor showed him a cell whose floor, walls, and vaulted ceiling were covered by a drawing (in barbaric colors that time, before obliterating, had refined) of an infinite tiger. It was a tiger composed of many tigers, in the most dizzying of ways; it was crisscrossed with tigers, striped with tigers, and contained seas and Himalayas and armies that resembled other tigers. The painter, a fakir, had died many years before, in that same cell; he had come from Sind or perhaps Gujarat and his initial purpose had been to draw a map of the world. Of that first purpose there remained some vestiges within the monstrous image. Taylor told this story to Muhammad al-Yemeni, of Fort William; al-Yemeni said that there was no creature in the world that did not tend toward becoming a *Zaheer*,[1] but that the All-Merciful does not allow two things to be a *Zaheer* at the same time, since a single one is capable of entrancing multitudes. He said that there is always a Zahir—in the Age of Ignorance it was the idol called Yahuk, and then a prophet from Khorasan who wore a veil spangled with precious stones or a mask of gold.[2] He also noted that Allah was inscrutable.

Over and over I read Barlach's monograph. I cannot sort out my emotions; I recall my desperation when I realized that nothing could any longer save me, the inward relief of knowing that I was not to blame for my misfortune, the envy I felt for those whose Zahir was not a coin but a slab of marble or a tiger. How easy it is not to think of a tiger!, I recall thinking. I also recall the remarkable uneasiness I felt when I read this paragraph: "One commentator of the *Gulshan i Raz* states that 'he who has seen the Zahir soon shall see the Rose' and quotes a line of poetry interpolated into Attar's *Asrar Nama* ('The Book of Things Unknown'): 'the Zahir is the shadow of the Rose and the rending of the Veil.'"

On the night of Teodelina's wake, I had been surprised not to see among those present Sra. Abascal, her younger sister. In October, I ran into a friend of hers.

1. This is Taylor's spelling of the word.
2. Barlach observes that Yahuk figures in the Qur'ān (71:23) and that the prophet is al-Moqanna (the Veiled Prophet) and that no one, with the exception of the surprising correspondent Philip Meadows Taylor, has ever linked those two figures to the Zahir.

"Poor Julita," the woman said to me, "she's become so odd. She's been put into Bosch.* How she must be crushed by those nurses' spoon-feeding her! She's still going on and on about that coin, just like Morena Sackmann's chauffeur."

Time, which softens recollections, only makes the memory of the Zahir all the sharper. First I could see the face of it, then the reverse; now I can see both sides at once. It is not as though the Zahir were made of glass, since one side is not superimposed upon the other—rather, it is as though the vision were itself spherical, with the Zahir rampant in the center. Anything that is not the Zahir comes to me as though through a filter, and from a distance—Teodelina's disdainful image, physical pain. Tennyson said that if we could but understand a single flower we might know who we are and what the world is. Perhaps he was trying to say that there is nothing, however humble, that does not imply the history of the world and its infinite concatenation of causes and effects. Perhaps he was trying to say that the visible world can be seen entire in every image, just as Schopenhauer tells us that the Will expresses itself entire in every man and woman. The Kabbalists believed that man is a microcosm, a symbolic mirror of the universe; if one were to believe Tennyson, *everything* would be—*everything*, even the unbearable Zahir.

Before the year 1948, Julia's fate will have overtaken me. I will have to be fed and dressed, I will not know whether it's morning or night, I will not know who the man Borges was. Calling that future terrible is a fallacy, since none of the future's circumstances will in any way affect me. One might as well call "terrible" the pain of an anesthetized patient whose skull is being trepanned. I will no longer perceive the universe, I will perceive the Zahir. Idealist doctrine has it that the verbs "to live" and "to dream" are at every point synonymous; for me, thousands upon thousands of appearances will pass into one; a complex dream will pass into a simple one. Others will dream that I am mad, while I dream of the Zahir. When every man on earth thinks, day and night, of the

Zahir, which will be dream and which reality, the earth or the Zahir?

In the waste and empty hours of the night I am still able to walk through the streets. Dawn often surprises me upon a bench in the Plaza Garay, thinking (or trying to think) about that passage in the *Asrar Nama* where it is said that the Zahir is the shadow of the Rose and the rending of the Veil. I link that pronouncement to this fact: In order to lose themselves in God, the Sufis repeat their own name or the ninety-nine names of God until the names mean nothing anymore. I long to travel that path. Perhaps by thinking about the Zahir unceasingly, I can manage to wear it away; perhaps behind the coin is God.

For Wally Zenner

The Writing of the God

The cell is deep and made of stone; its shape is that of an almost perfect hemisphere, although the floor (which is also of stone) is something less than a great circle, and this fact somehow deepens the sense of oppression and vastness. A wall divides the cell down the center; though it is very high, it does not touch the top of the vault. I, Tzinacán, priest of the Pyramid of Qaholom, which Pedro de Alvarado burned, am on one side of the wall; on the other there is a jaguar, which with secret, unvarying paces measures the time and space of its captivity. At floor level, a long window with thick iron bars interrupts the wall. At the shadowless hour [midday] a small door opens above us, and a jailer (whom the years have gradually blurred) operates an iron pulley, lowering to us, at the end of a rope, jugs of water and hunks of meat. Light enters the vault; it is then that I am able to see the jaguar.

I have lost count of the years I have lain in this darkness; I who once was young and could walk about this prison do nothing now but wait, in the posture of my death, for the end the gods have destined for me. With the deep flint blade I have opened the breast of victims, but now I could not, without the aid of magic, lift my own body from the dust.

On the day before the burning of the Pyramid, the men who got down from their high horses scourged me with burning irons, to compel me to reveal the site of a buried treasure. Before my eyes they toppled the idol to the god, yet the god did not abandon me, and I held my silence through their tortures. They tore my flesh, they crushed me, they mutilated me, and then I awoke in this prison, which I will never leave alive.

Driven by the inevitability of doing *something*, of somehow filling time, I tried, in my darkness, to remember everything I knew. I squandered entire nights in remembering the order and the number of certain stone serpents, or the shape of a medicinal tree. Thus did I gradually conquer the years, thus did I gradually come to possess those things I no longer possessed. One night I sensed that a precise recollection was upon me; before the traveler sees the ocean, he feels a stirring in his blood. Hours later, I began to make out the memory; it was one of the legends of the god. On the first day of creation, foreseeing that at the end of time many disasters and calamities would befall, the god had written a magical phrase, capable of warding off those evils. He wrote it in such a way that it would pass down to the farthest generations, and remain untouched by fate. No one knows where he wrote it, or with what letters, but we do know that it endures, a secret text, and that one of the elect shall read it. I reflected that we were, as always, at the end of time, and that it would be my fate, as the last priest of the god, to be afforded the privilege of intuiting those words. The fact that I was bounded within a cell did not prevent me from harboring that hope; I might have seen Qaholom's inscription thousands of times, and need only to understand it.

That thought gave me spirit, and then filled me with a kind of vertigo. In the wide realm of the world there are ancient forms, incorruptible and eternal forms—any one of them might be the symbol that I sought. A mountain might be the word of the god, or a river or the empire or the arrangement of the stars. And yet, in the course of the centuries mountains are leveled and the path of a river is many times diverted, and empires know mutability and ruin, and the design of the stars is altered. In the firmament there is change. The mountain and the star are individuals, and the life of an individual runs out. I sought something more tenacious, more invulnerable. I thought of the generations of grain, of grasses, of birds, of men. Perhaps the spell was written upon my very face, perhaps I myself was the object of my search. Amid those keen imaginings was I when I recalled that one of the names of the god was jaguar—*tigre.*

At that, my soul was filled with holiness. I imagined to myself the first morning of time, imagined my god entrusting the message to the living flesh of the jaguars, who would love one another and engender one another endlessly, in caverns, in cane fields, on islands, so that the last men might receive it. I imagined to myself that web of tigers, that hot labyrinth of tigers, bringing terror to the plains and pastures in order to preserve the design. In the other cell, there was a jaguar; in its proximity I sensed a confirmation of my conjecture, and a secret blessing.

Long years I devoted to learning the order and arrangement of the spots on the tiger's skin. During the course of each blind day I was granted an instant of light, and thus was I able to fix in my mind the black shapes that mottled the yellow skin. Some made circles; others formed transverse stripes on the inside of its legs; others, ringlike, occurred over and over again—perhaps they were the same sound, or the same word. Many had red borders.

I will not tell of the difficulties of my labor. More than once I cried out to the vault above that it was impossible to decipher that text. Gradually, I came to be tormented less by the concrete enigma which occupied my mind than by the generic enigma of a message written by a god. What sort of sentence, I asked myself, would be constructed by an absolute mind? I reflected that even in the languages of humans there is no proposition that does not imply the entire universe; to say "the jaguar" is to say all the jaguars that engendered it, the deer and turtles it has devoured, the grass that fed the deer, the earth that was mother to the grass, the sky that gave light to the earth. I reflected that in the language of a god every word would speak that infinite concatenation of events, and not implicitly but explicitly, and not linearly but instantaneously. In time, the idea of a divine utterance came to strike me as puerile, or as blasphemous. A god, I reflected, must speak but a single word, and in that word there must be *absolute plenitude*. No word uttered by a god could be less than the universe, or briefer than the sum of time. The ambitions and poverty of human words—*all, world, universe*—are but shadows or simulacra of that Word which is the equivalent of a language and all that can be comprehended within a language.

One day or one night—between my days and nights, what difference can there be?—I dreamed that there was a grain of sand on the floor of my cell. Unconcerned, I went back to sleep; I dreamed that I woke up and there were two grains of sand. Again I slept; I dreamed that now there were three. Thus the grains of sand multiplied, little by little, until they filled the cell and I was dying beneath that hemisphere of sand. I realized that I was dreaming; with a vast effort I woke myself. But waking up was useless—I was suffocated by the countless sand. Someone said to me: *You have wakened not out of sleep, but into a prior dream, and that dream lies within another, and so on, to infinity, which is the number of the grains of sand. The path that you are to take is endless, and you will die before you have truly awakened.*

I felt lost. The sand crushed my mouth, but I cried out: *I cannot be killed by sand that I dream—nor is there any such thing as a dream within a dream.* A bright light woke me. In the darkness above me, there hovered a circle of light. I saw the face and hands of the jailer, the pulley, the rope, the meat, and the water jugs.

Little by little, a man comes to resemble the shape of his destiny; a man *is*, in the long run, his circumstances. More than a decipherer or an avenger, more than a priest of the god, I was a prisoner. Emerging from that indefatigable labyrinth of dreams, I returned to my hard prison as though I were a man returning home. I blessed its dampness, I blessed its tiger, I blessed its high opening and the light, I blessed my old and aching body, I blessed the darkness and the stone.

And at that, something occurred which I cannot forget and yet cannot communicate—there occurred union with the deity, union with the universe (I do not know whether there is a difference between those two words). Ecstasy does not use the same symbol twice; one man has seen God in a blinding light, another has perceived Him in a sword or in the circles of a rose. I saw a Wheel of enormous height, which was not before my eyes, or behind them, or to the sides, but everywhere at once. This Wheel was made of water, but also of fire, and although I could see its boundaries, it was infinite. It was made of all things that shall be, that are, and that have been, all intertwined, and I was one of the strands within that all-encompassing fabric, and Pedro de Alvarado, who had tortured me, was another. In it were the causes and the effects, and the mere sight of that Wheel enabled me to understand all things, without end. O joy of understanding, greater than the joy of imagining, greater than the joy of feeling! I saw the universe and saw its secret designs. I saw the origins told by the Book of the People. I saw the mountains that rose from the water, saw the first men of wood, saw the water jars that turned against the men, saw the dogs that tore at their faces.* I saw the faceless god who is behind the gods. I saw the infinite processes that shape a single happiness, and, understanding all, I also came to understand the writing on the tiger.

It is a formula of fourteen random (apparently random) words, and all I would have to do to become omnipotent is speak it aloud. Speaking it would make this stone prison disappear, allow the day to enter my night, make me young, make me immortal, make the jaguar destroy Alvarado, bury the sacred blade in Spanish breasts, rebuild the Pyramid, rebuild the empire. Forty syllables, fourteen words, and I, Tzinacán, would rule the lands once ruled by Moctezuma. But I know that I shall never speak those words, because I no longer remember Tzinacán.

Let the mystery writ upon the jaguars die with me. He who has glimpsed the universe, he who has glimpsed the burning designs of the universe, can have no thought for a man, for a man's trivial joys or calamities, though he himself be that man. He *was* that man, who no longer matters to him. What does he care about the fate of that other man, what does he care about the other man's nation, when now he is no one? That is why I do not speak the formula, that is why, lying in darkness, I allow the days to forget me.

For Ema Risso Platero

Ibn-Hakam al-Bokhari, Murdered in His Labyrinth

. . . is the likeness of the spider who buildeth her a house.
Qur'ān, XXIX: 40

"This," said Dunraven with a vast gesture that did not blench at the cloudy stars, and that took in the black moors, the sea, and a majestic, tumbledown edifice that looked much like a stable fallen upon hard times, "is my ancestral land."

Unwin, his companion, removed the pipe from his mouth and uttered modest sounds of approbation. It was the first evening of the summer of 1914; weary of a world that lacked the dignity of danger, the friends prized the solitude of that corner of Cornwall. Dunraven cultivated a dark beard and was conscious of himself as the author of quite a respectable epic, though his contemporaries were incapable of so much as scanning it and its subject had yet to be revealed to him; Unwin had published a study of the theorem that Fermat had not written in the margins of a page by Diophantus. Both men—is there really any need to say this?—were young, absentminded, and passionate.

"It must be a good quarter century ago now," said Dunraven, "that Ibn-Hakam al-Bokhari, the chieftain or king or whatnot of some tribe or another along the Nile, died in the central chamber of that house at the hands of his cousin Sa'īd. Even after all these years, the circumstances of his death are still not entirely clear."

Meekly, Unwin asked why.

"Several reasons," came the answer. "First, that house up there

95

is a labyrinth. Second, a slave and a lion had stood guard over it. Third, a secret treasure disappeared—*poof!*, vanished. Fourth, the murderer was already dead by the time the murder took place. Fifth . . ."

Vexed a bit, Unwin stopped him.

"Please—let's not multiply the mysteries," he said. "Mysteries ought to be simple. Remember Poe's purloined letter, remember Zangwill's locked room."

"Or complex," volleyed Dunraven. "Remember the universe."

Climbing up steep sandy hills, they had arrived at the labyrinth. Seen at close range, it looked like a straight, virtually interminable wall of unplastered brick, scarcely taller than a man. Dunraven said it made a circle, but one so broad that its curvature was imperceptible. Unwin recalled Nicholas of Cusa, for whom every straight line was the arc of an infinite circle. . . .Toward midnight, they came upon a ruined doorway, which opened onto a long, perilous entryway whose walls had no other windows or doors. Dunraven said that inside, one came to crossing after crossing in the halls, but if they always turned to the left, in less than an hour they would be at the center of the maze. Unwin nodded. Their cautious steps echoed on the stone floor; at every branching, the corridor grew narrower. They felt they were being suffocated by the house—the ceiling was very low. They were forced to walk in single file through the knotted darkness. Unwin led the way; the invisible wall, cumbered with ruggedness and angles, passed endlessly under his hand. And as he made his way slowly through the darkness, Unwin heard from his friend's lips the story of Ibn-Hakam's death.

"What well may be my earliest memory," Dunraven began, "is Ibn-Hakam on the docks at Pentreath. He was followed by a black man with a lion—undoubtedly the first black man and the first lion I'd ever set eyes upon, with the exception of those lithographs of Bible stories, I suppose. I was just a boy then, but I'll tell you, that savage sun-colored beast and night-colored man didn't make the impression on me that Ibn-Hakam did. He seemed so tall. He was a sallow-skinned fellow, with black eyes and drooping eyelids, an insolent nose, thick lips, a saffron yellow beard, a broad chest, and a silent, self-assured way of walking. When I got home, I said, 'A king has come in a ship.' Later, when the brickmasons went to work, I expanded upon the title a bit and called him the King of Babel.

"The news that this outsider was to settle in Pentreath was welcome, I must say; the size and design of his house, though, met with amazement and even outrage. It seemed intolerable that a house should be composed of a single room, yet league upon league of hallways. 'That's all very well for the Moors,' people said, 'but no Christian ever built such a house.' Our rector, Mr. Allaby, a man of curious reading, dug up the story of a king punished by the Deity for having built a labyrinth, and he read it from the pulpit. The Monday following, Ibn-Hakam paid a visit to the rectory; the details of their brief interview were not made public at the time, but no sermon afterward ever alluded to the act of arrogance, and the Moor was able to hire his brickmasons. Years later, when Ibn-Hakam was murdered, Allaby gave a statement to the authorities as to the substance of their conversation.

"The words, he said, that Ibn-Hakam had stood in his study—not sat, mind you, but *stood*—and spoken to him were these, or words very similar: 'There is no longer any man who can contemn what I do. The sins that bring dishonor to my name are so terrible that even should I repeat the Ultimate Name of God for century upon century I would not succeed in mitigating even one of the torments that shall be mine; the sins that bring dishonor to my name are so terrible that even should I kill you with these very hands, that act would not increase the torments to which infinite Justice has destined me. There is no land ignorant of my name; I am Ibn-Hakam al-Bokhari, and I have ruled the tribes of the desert with an iron scepter. For many years with the aid of my cousin Sa'īd I plundered those tribes, but God hearkened to their

cries and suffered them to rise against me. My men were crushed
and put to the knife. I managed to flee with the treasure I had
hoarded up through my years of pillaging. Sa'īd led me to the
sepulcher of a saint, which lay at the foot of a stone mountain. I
ordered my slave man to stand watch over the face of the desert;
Sa'īd and I, exhausted, lay down to sleep. That night I dreamt
that I was imprisoned within a nest of vipers. I awoke in horror;
beside me, in the morning light, Sa'īd lay sleeping; the brush of
a spiderweb against my skin had caused me to dream that dream.
It pained me that Sa'īd, who was a coward, should sleep so
soundly. I reflected that the treasure was not infinite, and that he
might claim a part of it. In my waistband was my dagger with its
silver handle; I unsheathed it and drew it across his throat. As he
died he stammered out a few words that I could not understand.
I looked at him; he was dead, but I feared that he might yet stand,
so I ordered my slave to crush his face with a stone. After that,
we wandered under the heavens until one day we glimpsed a sea,
with tall ships furrowing its waves. The thought came to me that
a dead man cannot travel across the water, so I resolved to seek
out other lands. The first night that we were upon the ocean I
dreamt that I was murdering Sa'īd. Everything happened again,
just as it had before, but this time I understood his words. He said
As you slay me now, so shall I slay you, no matter where you flee. I have
sworn to foil that threat; I shall hide myself in the center of a
labyrinth, so that his shade may lose its way.'

"That said, Ibn-Hakam took his leave. Allaby tried to think
that the Moor was mad and that that absurd labyrinth of his was
a symbol, a clear testament to his madness. Then he reflected that
the notion of madness squared with the extravagant house and
the extravagant tale, but not with the lively impression that the
man Ibn-Hakam himself gave. Perhaps such tales were indigenous
to the sandy wastes of Egypt, perhaps such oddities, like the
dragons in Pliny, were attributable less to an individual person
than to a whole culture. . . .In London, Allaby pored through

back issues of the *Times*; he found that such a rebellion had in fact occurred, as had the subsequent defeat of al-Bokhari and his vizier, a man with a reputation as a coward.

"The moment the brickmasons were done, Ibn-Hakam set up housekeeping in the center of his labyrinth. He was never seen again by the townspeople; sometimes Allaby feared that Sa'īd had already gotten to him and killed him. At night, the wind would bring us the sound of the lion's roaring, and the sheep in the pen would huddle together in ancestral fear.

"Ships from Eastern ports would often anchor in our little bay here, bound for Cardiff or Bristol. The slave would come down from the labyrinth (which at that time, I recall, was not pink but bright crimson) and exchange African words with the crews; he seemed to be looking out for the vizier's ghost among the men. Everyone knew that these ships carried contraband, and if they were carrying outlawed ivories or liquors, why not the ghosts of dead men?

"Three years after the house was built, the *Rose of Sharon* anchored at the foot of the cliffs. I was not one of those who saw the ship, so it's altogether possible that the image I have of her is influenced by some forgotten print of Aboukir or Trafalgar, but my understanding is that she was one of those very elaborately carved vessels that seem less the work of shipwrights than of carpenters, and less that of carpenters than of cabinetmakers. She was (if not in reality, at least in my dreams) a burnished, dark, silent, swift craft, manned by Arabs and Malays.

"She anchored around dawn one morning in October. Toward nightfall, Ibn-Hakam burst into Allaby's house, totally unmanned by terror. He could hardly manage to tell Allaby that Sa'īd had found his way into the labyrinth, and that his slave and lion had been murdered. He asked in all seriousness if the authorities could do nothing to protect him. Before Allaby could answer, he was gone, for the second and last time—as though snatched away by the same terror that had brought him to the house. Sitting there

99

alone now in his study, Allaby thought with amazement that this terrified man had brought iron tribes in the Sudan under his thumb, had known what it is to do battle and what it is to kill. The next day, he noticed that the ship had sailed (for Suakin in the Red Sea, it was later learned). It occurred to him that it was his duty to confirm the murder of the slave, and so he climbed up to the labyrinth. Al-Bokhari's breathless story had sounded like mad fantasy to him, but at one corner in the long corridors he came upon the lion, which was dead, and at another, he found the slave, who was dead, and in the central chamber, he found Al-Bokhari himself, whose face had been smashed in. At the man's feet there was a coffer inlaid with mother-of-pearl; the lock had been forced and not a single coin remained."

The final periods, weighted with oratorical pauses, strained for eloquence; Unwin figured Dunraven had pronounced them many times, with the same self-conscious gravity and the same paucity of effect.

"How were the lion and the slave killed?" he asked, to feign interest.

The incorrigible voice answered with somber satisfaction.

"Their faces had been smashed in, as well."

To the sound of their footsteps was added the sound of rain. It occurred to Unwin that they would have to sleep in the labyrinth, in the central chamber of the tale, and that in retrospect he would surely see that long discomfort as adventure. He remained silent. Dunraven could not contain himself; like a man who will not forgive a debt, he asked:

"Quite an inexplicable story, don't you think?"

Unwin answered as though thinking out loud:

"I don't know whether it's explicable or inexplicable. I know it's a bloody lie."

Dunraven burst forth in a torrent of curses and invoked the eyewitness of the rector's elder son—Allaby, apparently, having died—and of every inhabitant of Pentreath. No less taken aback than Dunraven must have been, Unwin begged his pardon. Time, in the dark, seemed slower, longer; both men feared they had lost their way, and they were very tired by the time a dim brightness coming from above showed them the first steps of a narrow staircase. They climbed the stairs and found themselves in a round apartment, a good bit run-down and gone to seed. Two signs of the ill-fated king remained: a narrow window that looked out over the moors and the sea, and, in the floor, the trap door that opened onto the curve of the staircase. The apartment, though spacious, was very much like a jail cell.

Driven to it less by the rain than by the desire to live for the memory and the anecdote, the friends did spend the night within the labyrinth. The mathematician slept soundly; not so the poet, who was haunted by lines of poetry that his rational mind knew to be dreadful:

> *Faceless the sultry and overpowering lion,*
> *Faceless the stricken slave, faceless the king.*

Unwin had thought that the story of Al-Bokhari's murder held no interest for him, yet he awoke convinced that he had solved it. All that day he was preoccupied and taciturn, fitting and refitting the pieces, and two nights later, he rang up Dunraven and asked him to meet him at a pub in London, where he spoke to him these words, or words very much like them:

"Back in Cornwall, I said the story that you'd told me was a lie. What I meant was this: the *facts* were true, or might be true, but told in the way you told them, they were clearly humbug. Let me begin with the biggest lie of all, the incredible labyrinth. A fleeing man doesn't hide out in a labyrinth. He doesn't throw up a labyrinth on the highest point on the coast, and he doesn't throw up a crimson-colored labyrinth that sailors see from miles offshore. There's no need to build a labyrinth when the entire universe is one. For the man who truly wants to hide himself,

London is a much better labyrinth than a rooftop room to which every blessèd hallway in a building leads. That piece of wisdom, which I submit to you this evening, came to me night before last, while we were listening to the rain on the roof of the labyrinth and waiting to be visited by Morpheus. Warned and corrected by it, I chose to ignore those absurd 'facts' of yours and think about something sensible."

"Set theory, for instance, or the fourth dimension of space," Dunraven remarked.

"No," said Unwin with gravity. "I thought about the Cretan labyrinth. The labyrinth at whose center was a man with the head of a bull."

Dunraven, who had read a great many detective novels, thought that the solution of a mystery was always a good deal less interesting than the mystery itself; the mystery had a touch of the supernatural and even the divine about it, while the solution was a sleight of hand. In order to postpone the inevitable, he said:

"A bull's head is how the Minotaur appears on medals and in sculpture. Dante imagined it the other way around, with the body of a bull and the head of a man."

"That version works just as well," Unwin agreed. "What's important is the correspondence between the monstrous house and the monstrous creature that lives inside it. The Minotaur more than justifies the existence of the labyrinth—but no one can say the same for a threat dreamed in a dream. Once one seizes upon the image of the Minotaur (an image that's unavoidable when there's a labyrinth in the case) the problem is all but solved. I do have to confess, however, that I didn't see that that ancient image was the key to it, which is why it was necessary for your story to furnish me with a better, a more exact, symbol—the spiderweb."

"The spiderweb?" Dunraven repeated, perplexed.

"Yes. I shouldn't be surprised that the spiderweb (the universal form of the spiderweb, I mean—the Platonic spiderweb) suggested the crime to the murderer (because there *is* a murderer).

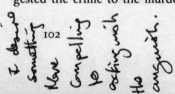

102

You'll recall that Al-Bokhari, in a tomb, dreamt of a nest of vipers and awoke to discover that a spiderweb had suggested the dream to him. Let's return to that night on which Al-Bokhari dreamt of the tangled nest. The overthrown king and the vizier and the slave are fleeing through the desert with a treasure. They take refuge in a tomb. The vizier—whom we know to be a coward—sleeps; the king—whom we know to be a brave man—does not. So as not to have to share the treasure with his vizier, the king stabs him to death; nights later, the murdered man's ghost threatens the king in a dream. None of this is to be believed; in my view, the events occurred exactly the other way around. That night, I believe, it was the king, the brave man, that slept, and Sa'īd, the coward, that lay awake. To sleep is to put the universe for a little while out of your mind, and that sort of unconcern is not easy for a man who knows that unsheathed swords are after him. Sa'īd, a greedy man, watched over the sleep of his king. He thought of killing him, perhaps even toyed with the knife, but he didn't have the courage for it. He called the slave. They hid part of the treasure in the tomb, then fled to Suakin and on to England. Not to hide from Al-Bokhari, you understand, but in fact to lure him to them and kill him—that was what led the vizier to build the high labyrinth of bright crimson walls in full view of the sea. He knew that ships would carry the fame of the slave, the lion, and the scarlet man back to the ports of Nubia, and that sooner or later Al-Bokhari would come to beard him in his labyrinth. The trap was laid in the web's last corridor. Al-Bokhari had infinite contempt for Sa'īd; he would never stoop to take the slightest precaution. The long-awaited day at last arrives; Ibn-Hakam disembarks in England, walks up to the door of the labyrinth, passes through the blind corridors, and has perhaps set his foot upon the first steps of the staircase when his vizier kills him—perhaps with a bullet, I don't know—from the trap door above. Then the slave no doubt killed the lion, and another bullet no doubt killed the slave. Then Sa'īd smashed in the three faces with a large rock. He had to do that; a single dead man with his face smashed in would have suggested a problem of identity, but the lion, the black man, and the king were elements in a series whose first terms would lead inevitably to the last. There's nothing strange about the fact that the man that visited Allaby was seized with terror; he had just committed the dreadful deed and was about to flee England and recover his treasure."

A thoughtful, or incredulous, silence followed Unwin's words. Dunraven called for another mug of ale before he offered his opinion.

"I accept," he said, "that my Ibn-Hakam might be Sa'īd. Such metamorphoses, you will tell me, are classic artifices of the genre—conventions that the reader insists be followed. What I hesitate to accept is the hypothesis that part of the treasure was left behind in the Sudan. Remember that Sa'īd was fleeing the king *and the enemies of the king, as well*; it's easier, it seems to me, to imagine him stealing the entire treasure than taking the time to bury part of it. Perhaps no odd coins were found lying about because there were no coins left; perhaps the brickmasons had consumed a treasure which, unlike the gold of the Nibelungen, was not infinite. Thus we would have Ibn-Hakam crossing the sea to reclaim a squandered treasure."

"Not *squandered*," said Unwin. "Invested. Invested in erecting upon the soil of infidels a great circular trap of brickwork intended to entangle and annihilate the king. Sa'īd's actions, if your supposition is correct, were motivated not by greed but by hatred and fear. He stole the treasure and then realized that the treasure was not for him the essential thing. The essential thing was that Ibn-Hakam die. He pretended to be Ibn-Hakam, killed Ibn-Hakam, and at last *was* Ibn-Hakam."

"Yes," agreed Dunraven. "He was a wanderer who, before becoming no one in death, would recall once having been a king, or having pretended to be a king."

The Two Kings and the Two Labyrinths[1]

It is said by men worthy of belief (though Allah's knowledge is greater) that in the first days there was a king of the isles of Babylonia who called together his architects and his priests and bade them build him a labyrinth so confused and so subtle that the most prudent men would not venture to enter it, and those who did would lose their way. Most unseemly was the edifice that resulted, for it is the prerogative of God, not man, to strike confusion and inspire wonder. In time there came to the court a king of the Arabs, and the king of Babylonia (to mock the simplicity of his guest) bade him enter the labyrinth, where the king of the Arabs wandered, humiliated and confused, until the coming of the evening, when he implored God's aid and found the door. His lips offered no complaint, though he said to the king of Babylonia that in his land he had another labyrinth, and Allah willing, he would see that someday the king of Babylonia made its acquaintance. Then he returned to Arabia with his captains and his wardens and he wreaked such havoc upon the kingdoms of Babylonia, and with such great blessing by fortune, that he brought low its castles, crushed its people, and took the king of Babylonia himself captive. He tied him atop a swift-footed camel and led him into the desert. Three days they rode, and then he said to him, "O king of time and substance and cipher of the century! In Babylonia didst thou attempt to make me lose my way

[1]. This is the story read by the rector from his pulpit. See p. 97.

105

in a labyrinth of brass with many stairways, doors, and walls; now the Powerful One has seen fit to allow me to show thee mine, which has no stairways to climb, nor doors to force, nor wearying galleries to wander through, nor walls to impede thy passage."

Then he untied the bonds of the king of Babylonia and abandoned him in the middle of the desert, where he died of hunger and thirst. Glory to Him who does not die.

The Wait

The coach left him at number 4004 on that street in the northwest part of the city. It was not yet 9:00 A.M.; the man noted with approval the mottled plane trees, the square of dirt at the foot of each, the decent houses with their little balconies, the pharmacy next door, the faded diamonds of the paint store and the hardware store. A long windowless hospital wall abutted the sidewalk across the street; farther down, the sun reflected off some greenhouses. It occurred to the man that those things (now arbitrary, coincidental, and in no particular order, like things seen in dreams) would in time, God willing, become unchanging, necessary, and familiar. In the pharmacy window, porcelain letters spelled out "Breslauer": the Jews were crowding out the Italians, who had crowded out the native-born. All the better: the man preferred not to mix with people of his own blood.

The coachman helped him lift down his trunk; a distracted- or weary-looking woman finally opened the door. From the driver's seat, the coachman handed the man back one of the coins, a Uruguayan two-centavo piece that had been in the man's pocket since that night in the hotel in Melo. The man gave him forty centavos, and instantly regretted it: "I must act so that everyone will forget me. I've made two mistakes: I've paid with a coin from another country and I've let this man see that the mistake matters."

Preceded by the woman, the man walked through the long entryway and on through the first patio; the room he'd reserved was, as good luck would have it, off the second patio, in the rear.

There was a bed of ironwork that art had distorted into fantastic curves suggesting vines and branches; there were also a tall pine chifforobe, a night table, a bookcase with books on the bottommost shelf, two mismatched chairs, and a washstand with its bowl, pitcher, and soap dish and a carafe of cloudy glass. A crucifix and a map of Buenos Aires province adorned the walls; the wallpaper was crimson, with a pattern of large peacocks, tails outspread. The room's only door opened onto the patio. The chairs had to be rearranged to make room for the trunk. The tenant gave his nod to everything; when the woman asked him what his name was, he said Villari—not as a secret act of defiance, not to mitigate a humiliation that quite honestly he didn't feel, but rather because that name haunted him, he couldn't come up with another one. Certainly he was not seduced by the literary error of imagining that adopting the name of his enemy would be the astute thing to do.

At first Sr. Villari never left the house, but after a few weeks had passed he started going out for a while at nightfall. In the evening he would occasionally go into the motion-picture theater three blocks away. He never sat nearer the screen than the last row; he always got up a little before the picture was over. He saw tragic stories of the underworld; no doubt they had their errors; no doubt they included certain images that were also a part of Sr. Villari's previous life, but he didn't notice the errors, because the notion that there might be parallels between art and life never occurred to him. He docilely tried to like things; he tried to take things in the spirit they were offered. Unlike people who had read novels, he never saw himself as a character in a book.

He never received a letter, or even a circular, but with vague hopefulness he read one of the sections of the newspaper. In the afternoon, he would draw one of the chairs over to the door and sit and sip gravely at his *mate*, his eyes fixed on the ivy that climbed the wall of the two-story house next door. Years of solitude had taught him that although in one's memory days all tend to be the same, there wasn't a day, even when a man was in jail or hospital, that didn't have its surprises. During other periods of isolation he had given in to the temptation to count the days (and even the hours), but this isolation was different, because there was no end to it—unless the newspaper should bring him news one morning of the death of Alejandro Villari. It was also possible that Villari *was already dead*, and then his life was a dream. That possibility disturbed him, because he couldn't quite figure out whether it felt like a relief or a misfortune; he told himself it was absurd, and he discarded it. In now-distant days—distant less because of the lapse of time than because of two or three irrevocable acts—he had desired many things, with a desire that lacked all scruples; that powerful urge to possess, which had inspired the hatred of men and the love of the occasional woman, no longer desired *things*—it wanted only to endure, wanted not to end. The taste of the *mate*, the taste of the black tobacco, the growing band of shade that slowly crept across the patio—these were reason enough to live.

There was a wolf-dog in the house, now grown quite old; Villari made friends with it. He spoke to it in Spanish, in Italian, and with the few words he still remembered of the rustic dialect of his childhood. Villari tried to live in the mere present, looking neither backward nor ahead; memories mattered less to him than his visions of the future. In some obscure way he thought he could sense that the past is the stuff that time is made of; that was why time became past so quickly. One day his weariness felt for a moment like happiness; at moments such as that, he was not a great deal more complex than the dog.

One night he was left shocked, speechless, and trembling by a burst of pain deep in his mouth, striking almost at the heart of him. Within a few minutes, that horrible miracle returned, and then again toward dawn. The next day Villari sent for a cab, which left him at a dentist's office in the neighborhood of Plaza del Once.* There, his tooth was pulled. At the "moment of truth," he was neither more cowardly nor more composed than anyone else.

Another night, as he came back from the motion-picture theater, he felt someone shove him. Furious, indignant, and with secret relief, he turned on the insolent culprit; he spit out a filthy insult. The other man, dumb-founded, stammered an apology. He was a tall young man with dark hair; on his arm was a German-looking woman. That night Villari told himself many times that he didn't know them; still, four or five days went by before he went out again.

Among the books in the bookcase was a *Divine Comedy*, with the old commentary by Andreoli. Impelled less by curiosity than by a sense of duty, Villari undertook to read that masterpiece. He would read a canto before dinner, and then, strictly and methodically, the notes. He did not think of the infernal torments as improbable or excessive, nor did it occur to him that Dante would have condemned him, Villari, to the farthest circle of Hell, where Ugolino's teeth gnaw endlessly at Ruggieri's throat.

The peacocks on the crimson wallpaper seemed the perfect thing for feeding persistent nightmares, but Sr. Villari never dreamed of a monstrous gazebo of living birds all intertangled. In the early-morning hours he would dream a dream of unvarying backdrop but varying details. Villari and two other men would come into a room with revolvers drawn, or he would be jumped by them as he came out of the motion-picture theater, or they— all three of them at once—would be the stranger that had shoved him, or they would wait for him sad-faced out in the courtyard and pretend not to know him. At the end of the dream, he would take the revolver out of the drawer in the nightstand that stood beside the bed (and there *was* a gun in that drawer) and fire it at the men. The noise of the gun would wake him, but it was always a dream—and in another dream the attack would occur again and in another dream he would have to kill them again.

One murky morning in July, the presence of strange people

(not the sound of the door when they opened it) woke him. Tall in the shadowy dimness of the room, oddly simplified by the dimness (in the frightening dreams, they had always been brighter), motionless, patient, and watching, their eyes lowered as though the weight of their weapons made them stoop-shouldered, Alejandro Villari and a stranger had at last caught up with him. He gestured at them to wait, and he turned over and faced the wall, as though going back to sleep. Did he do that to awaken the pity of the men that killed him, or because it's easier to endure a terrifying event than to imagine it, wait for it endlessly—or (and this is perhaps the most likely possibility) so that his murderers would become a dream, as they had already been so many times, in that same place, at that same hour?

That was the magic spell he was casting when he was rubbed out by the revolvers' fire.

The Man on the Threshold

Bioy Casares brought back a curious knife from London, with a triangular blade and an H-shaped hilt; our friend Christopher Dewey, of the British Council, said that sort of weapon was in common use in Hindustan. That verdict inspired him also to mention that he had once worked in Hindustan, between the two wars. (*Ultra aurorem et Gangem*, I recall him saying in Latin, misquoting a verse from Juvenal.) Among the stories he told us that night, I shall be so bold as to reconstruct the one that follows. My text will be a faithful one; may Allah prevent me from adding small circumstantial details or heightening the exotic lineaments of the tale with interpolations from Kipling. Besides, it has an antique, simple flavor about it that it would be a shame to lose— something of the *1001 Nights*.

The precise geography of the facts I am going to relate hardly matters. And besides—what sort of exactness can the names Amritsar and Udh be expected to convey in Buenos Aires? I shall only say, then, that back in those years there were riots in a certain Muslim city, and that the central government sent a strong fellow in to impose order. The man was a Scot, descended from an illustrious clan of warriors, and in his blood there flowed a history of violence. My eyes beheld him but one time, but I shall never forget the jet black hair, the prominent cheekbones, the avid nose and mouth, the broad shoulders, the strong Viking bones. David Alexander Glencairn shall be his name tonight in my story. The two Christian names befit the man, for they are the names of kings who ruled with an iron scepter. David Alexander Glencairn (I shall have to get used to calling him that) was, I suspect, a man who was greatly feared; the mere announcement of his coming was sufficient to cast peace over the city. That, however, did not keep him from putting into effect a number of forceful measures. Several years passed; the city and the district were at peace; Sikhs and Muslims had put aside their ancient discords. And then suddenly Glencairn disappeared. Naturally, there were any number of rumors of his having been kidnapped or killed.

These things I learned from my superior, because there was strict censorship and the newspapers didn't discuss Glencairn's disappearance—did not so much as mention it, so far as I can recall. There is a saying, you know—that India is larger than the world; Glencairn, who may have been all-powerful in the city to which he was fated by a signature at the end of some document, was a mere cipher in the coils and springs and workings of the Empire. The searches performed by the local police turned up nothing; my superior thought that a single individual, working on his own, might inspire less resentment and achieve better results. Three or four days later (distances in India are what one might call generous), I was working with no great hope through the streets of the opaque city that had magically swallowed up a man.

I felt, almost immediately, the infinite presence of a spell cast to hide Glencairn's whereabouts. *There is not a soul in this city* (I came to suspect) *that doesn't know the secret, and that hasn't sworn to keep it.* Most people, when I interrogated them, pleaded unbounded ignorance; they didn't know who Glencairn was, had never seen the man, never heard of him. Others, contrariwise, had seen him not a quarter of an hour ago talking to Such-and-such, and they would even show me the house the two men had gone into, where of course nobody knew a thing about them—or where I'd just missed them, they'd left just a minute earlier. More than once

I balled my fist and hit one of those tellers of precisely detailed lies smack in the face. Bystanders would applaud the way I got my frustrations off my chest, and then make up more lies. I didn't believe them, but I didn't dare ignore them. One evening somebody left me an envelope containing a slip of paper on which were written some directions. . . .

By the time I arrived, the sun had pretty well gone down. The neighborhood was one of common folk, the humble of the earth; the house was squat. From the walkway in the street I could make out a series of courtyards of packed earth and then, toward the rear, a brightness. Back in the last courtyard, some sort of Muslim celebration was going on; a blind man entered with a lute made of reddish-colored wood.

At my feet, on the threshold of this house, as motionless as an inanimate *thing*, a very old man lay curled up on the ground. I shall describe him, because he is an essential part of the story. His many years had reduced and polished him the way water smooths and polishes a stone or generations of men polish a proverb. He was covered in long tatters, or so it looked to me, and the turban that wound about his head looked frankly like one rag the more. In the fading evening light, he lifted his dark face and very white beard to me. I spoke to him without preamble—because I had already lost all hope, you see—about David Alexander Glencairn. He didn't understand me (or perhaps he didn't hear me) and I had to explain that Glencairn was a judge and that I was looking for him. When I uttered those words, I felt how absurd it was to question this ancient little man for whom the present was scarcely more than an indefinite rumor. *News of the Mutiny or the latest word of Akbar, this man might have* (I thought), *but not of Glencairn.* What he told me confirmed that suspicion.

"A judge!" he said with frail astonishment. "A judge who is lost and being searched for. The event took place when I was a boy. I know nothing of dates, but Nikal Seyn had not died at the wall at Delhi yet"—Nicholson he meant, you see. "The past lives on in memory; surely I shall be able to recover what in that time took place. Allah had permitted, in His wrath, that mankind grow corrupted; filled with curses were men's mouths, and with falsehoods and deception. And yet not all men were perverse, so that when it was proclaimed that the queen was going to send a man to enforce the laws of England in this land, the least evil of men were glad, because they felt that law is better than disorder. The Christian came, but no time did it take him to prevaricate and oppress, to find extenuation for abominable crimes, and to sell his verdicts. At first, we did not blame him; none of us were familiar with the English justice he administered, and for all we knew, this judge's seeming abuses were inspired by valid, though arcane, reasons. *Surely all things have justification in his book*, we tried to think, but his similarity to the other evil judges of the world was too clear, and at last we had to admit that he was simply an evil man. He soon became a tyrant, and my poor people (in order to avenge themselves for the mistaken hope that once they had reposed in him) came to entertain the idea of kidnapping him and putting him to trial. Talking was not sufficient; from fine words, it was necessary that we move onward to acts. No one, perhaps, with the exception of the simplest of mind or the youngest of years, believed that such a terrible purpose would ever be fulfilled, but thousands of Sikhs and Muslims kept their word, and one day, incredulous, they *did* what each of them had thought impossible. They kidnapped the judge, and for a prison they put him in a farmhouse in the distant outskirts of the town. Then they consulted with the subjects who had been aggrieved by him, or in some cases with the subjects' orphans and widows, for the executioner's sword had not rested during those years. At last—and this was perhaps the most difficult thing of all—they sought for and appointed a judge to judge the judge."

Here the man was interrupted by several women who made their way into the house. Then he went on, slowly:

"It is said that every generation of mankind includes four

honest men who secretly hold up the universe and justify it to the Lord. One of those men would have been the most fitting judge. But where was one to find them, if they wander the earth lost and anonymous and are not recognized when they are met with and not even they themselves know the high mission they perform? Someone, therefore, reflected that if fate had forbidden us wise men, we should seek out fools. That opinion won the day. Scholars of the Qur'ān, doctors of the law, Sikhs who bear the name of lions yet worship God, Hindus who worship a multitude of gods, monks of the master Mahavira who teach that the shape of the universe is that of a man with his legs spread open wide, worshipers of fire, and black Jews composed the tribunal, but the ultimate verdict was to be decided by a madman."

Here he was interrupted by several people leaving the celebration.

"A madman," he repeated, "so that the wisdom of God might speak through his mouth and bring shame to human pride and overweening. The name of this man has been lost, or perhaps was never known, but he wandered these streets naked, or covered with rags, counting his fingers with his thumb and hurling gibes at the trees."

My good sense rebelled. I said that to leave the decision to a madman was to make a mockery of the trial.

"The accused man accepted the judge," was the reply. "Perhaps he realized that given the fate that awaited the conspirators if they should set him free, it was only from a madman that he might hope for anything but a sentence of death. I have heard that he laughed when he was told who the judge was to be. The trial lasted for many days and nights, because of the great number of witnesses."

He fell silent. Some concern was at work in him. To break the silence, I asked how many days it had been.

"At least nineteen days," he replied. More people leaving the celebration interrupted him; Muslims are forbidden wine, but the faces and voices seemed those of drunkards. One of the men shouted something at the old man as he passed by.

"Nineteen days exactly," he emended. "The infidel dog heard the sentence, and the knife was drawn across his throat."

He spoke with joyous ferocity, but it was with another voice that he ended his story.

"He died without fear. Even in the basest of men there is some virtue."

"Where did this take place that you have told me about?" I asked him. "In a farmhouse?"

For the first time he looked me in the eye. Then slowly, measuring his words, he answered.

"I said a farmhouse was his prison, not that he was tried there. He was tried in this very city, in a house like all other houses, like this one. . . .One house is like another—what matters is knowing whether it is built in heaven or in hell."

I asked him what had happened to the conspirators.

"That, I do not know," he said patiently. "These things happened many years ago and by now they have been long forgotten. Perhaps they were condemned by men, but not by God."

Having said this he got up. I felt that his words dismissed me, that from that moment onward I had ceased to exist for him. A mob of men and women of all the nations of Punjab spilled out over us, praying and singing, and almost swept us away; I was astonished that such narrow courtyards, little more than long entryways, could have contained such numbers of people. Others came out of neighboring houses; no doubt they had jumped over the walls. . . .Pushing and shouting imprecations, I opened a way for myself. In the farthest courtyard I met a naked man crowned with yellow flowers, whom everyone was kissing and making obeisances to; there was a sword in his hand. The sword was bloody, for it had murdered Glencairn, whose mutilated body I found in the stables at the rear.

The Aleph

O God, I could be bounded in a nutshell and count myself a King of infinite space. Hamlet, II:2

But they will teach us that Eternity is the Standing still of the Present Time, a Nunc-stans *(as the Schools call it); which neither they, nor any else understand, no more than they would a* Hic-stans *for an Infinite greatnesse of Place.* Leviathan, IV:46

That same sweltering morning that Beatriz Viterbo died, after an imperious confrontation with her illness in which she had never for an instant stooped to either sentimentality or fear, I noticed that a new advertisement for some cigarettes or other (*blondes*, I believe they were) had been posted on the iron billboards of the Plaza Constitución; the fact deeply grieved me, for I realized that the vast unceasing universe was already growing away from her, and that this change was but the first in an infinite series. *The universe may change, but I shall not*, thought I with melancholy vanity. I knew that more than once my futile devotion had exasperated her; now that she was dead, I could consecrate myself to her memory—without hope, but also without humiliation. I reflected that April 30 was her birthday; stopping by her house on Calle Garay that day to pay my respects to her father and her first cousin Carlos Argentino Daneri was an irreproachable, perhaps essential act of courtesy. Once again I would wait in the

118

half-light of the little parlor crowded with furniture and draperies and bric-a-brac, once again I would study the details of the many photographs and portraits of her: Beatriz Viterbo, in profile, in color; Beatriz in a mask at the Carnival of 1921; Beatriz' first communion; Beatriz on the day of her wedding to Roberto Alessandri; Beatriz shortly after the divorce, lunching at the Jockey Club; Beatriz in Quilmes* with Delia San Marco Porcel and Carlos Argentino; Beatriz with the Pekinese that had been a gift from Villegas Haedo; Beatriz in full-front and in three-quarters view, smiling, her hand on her chin. . . .I would not be obliged, as I had been on occasions before, to justify my presence with modest offerings of books—books whose pages I learned at last to cut, so as not to find, months later, that they were still intact.

Beatriz Viterbo died in 1929; since then, I have not allowed an April 30 to pass without returning to her house. That first time, I arrived at seven-fifteen and stayed for about twenty-five minutes; each year I would turn up a little later and stay a little longer; in 1933, a downpour came to my aid: they were forced to ask me to dinner. Naturally, I did not let that fine precedent go to waste; in 1934 I turned up a few minutes after eight with a lovely confection from Santa Fe; it was perfectly natural that I should stay for dinner. And so it was that on those melancholy and vainly erotic anniversaries I came to receive the gradual confidences of Carlos Argentino Daneri.

Beatriz was tall, fragile, very slightly stooped; in her walk, there was (if I may be pardoned the oxymoron) something of a graceful clumsiness, a *soupçon* of hesitancy, or of palsy; Carlos Argentino is a pink, substantial, gray-haired man of refined features. He holds some sort of subordinate position in an illegible library in the outskirts toward the south of the city; he is authoritarian, though also ineffectual; until very recently he took advantage of nights and holidays to remain at home. At two generations' remove, the Italian *s* and the liberal Italian gesticulation still survive in him. His mental activity is constant, passionate, versatile, and utterly insignificant. He is full of pointless analogies and idle scruples. He has (as Beatriz did) large, beautiful, slender hands. For some months he labored under an obsession for Paul Fort, less for Fort's ballads than the idea of a glory that could never be tarnished. "He is the prince of the poets of *la belle France*," he would fatuously say. "You assail him in vain; you shall never touch him—not even the most venomous of your darts shall ever touch him."

On April 30, 1941, I took the liberty of enriching my sweet offering with a bottle of domestic brandy. Carlos Argentino tasted it, pronounced it "interesting," and, after a few snifters, launched into an *apologia* for modern man.

"I picture him," he said with an animation that was rather unaccountable, "in his study, as though in the watchtower of a great city, surrounded by telephones, telegraphs, phonographs, the latest in radio-telephone and motion-picture and magic-lantern equipment, and glossaries and calendars and timetables and bulletins. . . ."

He observed that for a man so equipped, the act of traveling was supererogatory; this twentieth century of ours had upended the fable of Muhammad and the mountain—mountains nowadays did in fact come to the modern Muhammad.

So witless did these ideas strike me as being, so sweeping and pompous the way they were expressed, that I associated them immediately with literature. Why, I asked him, didn't he write these ideas down? Predictably, he replied that he already had; they, and others no less novel, figured large in the Augural Canto, Prolingurial Canto, or simply Prologue-Canto, of a poem on which he had been working, with no deafening hurly-burly and *sans réclame*, for many years, leaning always on those twin staffs Work and Solitude. First he would open the floodgates of the imagination, then repair to the polishing wheel. The poem was entitled *The Earth*; it centered on a description of our own terraqueous orb and was graced, of course, with picturesque digression and elegant apostrophe.

I begged him to read me a passage, even if only a brief one. He opened a desk drawer, took out a tall stack of tablet paper stamped with the letterhead of the Juan Crisóstomo Lafinur Library,* and read, with ringing self-satisfaction:

> *I have seen, as did the Greek, man's cities and his fame,*
> *The works, the days of various light, the hunger;*
> *I prettify no fact, I falsify no name,*
> *For the* voyage *I narrate is* . . . autour de ma chambre.

"A stanza interesting from every point of view," he said. "The first line wins the kudos of the learned, the academician, the Hellenist—though perhaps not that of those would-be scholars that make up such a substantial portion of popular opinion. The second moves from Homer to Hesiod (implicit homage, at the very threshold of the dazzling new edifice, to the father of didactic poetry), not without revitalizing a technique whose lineage may be traced to Scripture—that is, enumeration, congeries, or conglobation. The third—baroque? decadent? the purified and fanatical cult of form?—consists of twinned hemistichs; the fourth, unabashedly bilingual, assures me the unconditional support of every spirit able to feel the ample attractions of playfulness. I shall say nothing of the unusual rhyme, nor of the erudition that allows me—without pedantry or boorishness!—to include within the space of four lines three erudite allusions spanning thirty centuries of dense literature: first the *Odyssey*, second the *Works and Days*, and third that immortal bagatelle that regales us with the diversions of the Savoyard's plume. . . .Once again, I show my awareness that truly *modern* art demands the balm of laughter, of *scherzo*. There is no doubt about it—Goldoni was right!"

Carlos Argentino read me many another stanza, all of which earned the same profuse praise and comment from him. There was nothing memorable about them; I could not even judge them to be much worse than the first one. Application, resignation, and chance had conspired in their composition; the virtues that Daneri attributed to them were afterthoughts. I realized that the poet's work had lain not in the poetry but in the invention of reasons for accounting the poetry admirable; naturally, that later work modified the poem for Daneri, but not for anyone else. His oral expression was extravagant; his metrical clumsiness prevented him, except on a very few occasions, from transmitting that extravagance to the poem.[1]

Only once in my lifetime have I had occasion to examine the fifteen thousand dodecasyllables of the *Polyalbion*—that topographical epic in which Michael Drayton recorded the fauna, flora, hydrography, orography, military and monastic history of England—but I am certain that Drayton's massive yet limited *œuvre* is less tedious than the vast enterprise conceived and given birth by Carlos Argentino. He proposed to versify the entire planet; by 1941 he had already dispatched several hectares of the state of Queensland, more than a kilometer of the course of the Ob, a gasworks north of Veracruz, the leading commercial establishments in the parish of Concepción, Mariana Cambaceres de Alvear's villa on Calle Once de Setiembre in Belgrano, and a Turkish bath not far from the famed Brighton Aquarium. He read me certain laborious passages from the Australian region of his

---

1. I do, however, recall these lines from a satire in which he lashed out vehemently against bad poets:

> This one fits the poem with a coat of mail
> Of erudition; that one, with gala pomps and circumstance.
> Both flail their absurd pennons to no avail,
> Neglecting, poor wretches, the factor sublime—its LOVELINESS!

It was only out of concern that he might create an army of implacable and powerful enemies, he told me, that he did not fearlessly publish the poem.

poem; his long, formless alexandrines lacked the relative agitation of the prologue. Here is one stanza:

> *Hear this. To the right hand of the routine signpost*
> *(Coming—what need is there to say?—from*
>   *north-northwest)*
> *Yawns a bored skeleton—Color? Sky-pearly.—*
> *Outside the sheepfold that suggests an ossuary.*

"Two audacious risks!" he exclaimed in exultation, "snatched from the jaws of disaster, I can hear you mutter, by success! I admit it, I admit it. One, the epithet *routine*, while making an adjective of a synonym for 'highway,' nods, *en passant*, to the inevitable tedium inherent to those chores of a pastoral and rustic nature that neither georgics nor our own belaureled *Don Segundo* ever dared acknowledge in such a forthright way, with no beating about the bush. And the second, delicately referring to the first, the forcefully prosaic phrase *Yawns a bored skeleton*, which the finicky will want to excommunicate without benefit of clergy but that the critic of more manly tastes will embrace as he does his very life. The entire line, in fact, is a good 24 karats. The second half-line sets up the most animated sort of conversation with the reader; it anticipates his lively curiosity, puts a question in his mouth, and then . . . *voilà*, answers it . . . on the instant. And what do you think of that coup *sky-pearly?* The picturesque neologism just *hints* at the sky, which is such an important feature of the Australian landscape. Without that allusion, the hues of the sketch would be altogether too gloomy, and the reader would be compelled to close the book, his soul deeply wounded by a black and incurable melancholy."

About midnight, I took my leave.

Two Sundays later, Daneri telephoned me for what I believe was the first time in his or my life. He suggested that we meet at four, "to imbibe the milk of the gods together in the nearby salon-bar that my estimable landlords, Messrs. Zunino and Zungri, have had the rare commercial foresight to open on the corner. It is a *café* you will do well to acquaint yourself with." I agreed, with more resignation than enthusiasm, to meet him. It was hard for us to find a table; the relentlessly modern "salon-bar" was only slightly less horrendous than I had expected; at neighboring tables, the excited clientele discussed the sums invested by Zunino and Zungri without a second's haggling. Carlos Argentino pretended to be amazed at some innovation in the establishment's lighting (an innovation he'd no doubt been apprised of beforehand) and then said to me somewhat severely:

"Much against your inclinations it must be that you recognize that this place is on a par with the most elevated heights of Flores."*

Then he reread four or five pages of his poem to me. Verbal ostentation was the perverse principle that had guided his revisions: where he had formerly written "blue" he now had "azure" "cerulean," and even "bluish." The word "milky" was not sufficiently hideous for him; in his impetuous description of a place where wool was washed, he had replaced it with "lactine," "lactescent," "lactoreous," "lacteal." . . . He railed bitterly against his critics; then, in a more benign tone, he compared them to those persons "who possess neither precious metals nor even the steam presses, laminators, and sulfuric acids needed for minting treasures, but who can *point out* to others the *precise location* of a treasure." Then he was off on another tack, inveighing against the obsession for forewords, what he called "prologomania," an attitude that "had already been spoofed in the elegant preface to the *Quixote* by the Prince of Wits himself." He would, however, admit that an attention-getting recommendation might be a good idea at the portals of his new work—"an accolade penned by a writer of stature, of real import." He added that he was planning to publish the first cantos of his poem. It was at that point that I understood the unprecedented telephone call and the invitation:

the man was about to ask me to write the preface to that pedantic farrago of his. But my fear turned out to be unfounded. Carlos Argentino remarked, with grudging admiration, that he believed he did not go too far in saying that the prestige achieved in every sphere by the man of letters Alvaro Melián Lafinur was "solid," and that if I could be persuaded to persuade him, Alvaro "might be enchanted to write the called-for foreword." In order to forestall the most unpardonable failure on my part, I was to speak on behalf of the poem's two incontrovertible virtues: its formal perfection and its scientific rigor—"because that broad garden of rhetorical devices, figures, charms, and graces will not tolerate a single detail that does not accord with its severe truthfulness." He added that Beatriz had always enjoyed Alvaro's company.

I agreed, I agreed most profusely. I did, however, for the sake of added plausibility, make it clear that I wouldn't be speaking with Alvaro on Monday but rather on Thursday, at the little supper that crowned each meeting of the Writers Circle. (There are no such suppers, although it is quite true that the meetings are held on Thursday, a fact that Carlos Argentino might verify in the newspapers and that lent a certain credence to my contention.) I told him (half-prophetically, half-farsightedly) that before broaching the subject of the prologue, I would describe the curious design of the poem. We said our good-byes; as I turned down Calle Bernardo de Irigoyen, I contemplated as impartially as I could the futures that were left to me: (a) speak with Alvaro and tell him that that first cousin of Beatriz' (the explanatory circumlocution would allow me to speak her name) had written a poem that seemed to draw out to infinity the possibilities of cacophony and chaos; (b) not speak with Alvaro. Knowing myself pretty well, I foresaw that my indolence would opt for (b).

From early Friday morning on, the telephone was a constant source of anxiety. I was indignant that this instrument from which Beatriz' irrecoverable voice had once emerged might now be reduced to transmitting the futile and perhaps angry complaints of that self-deluding Carlos Argentino Daneri. Fortunately, nothing came of it—save the inevitable irritation inspired by a man who had charged me with a delicate mission and then forgotten all about me.

Eventually the telephone lost its terrors, but in late October Carlos Argentino did call me. He was very upset; at first I didn't recognize his voice. Dejectedly and angrily he stammered out that that now unstoppable pair Zunino and Zungri, under the pretext of expanding their already enormous "*café*," were going to tear down his house.

"The home of my parents—the home where I was born—the old and deeply rooted house on Calle Garay!" he repeated, perhaps drowning his grief in the melodiousness of the phrase.

It was not difficult for me to share his grief. After forty, every change becomes a hateful symbol of time's passing; in addition, this was a house that I saw as alluding infinitely to Beatriz. I tried to make that extremely delicate point clear; my interlocutor cut me off. He said that if Zunino and Zungri persisted in their absurd plans, then Zunni, his attorney, would sue them *ipso facto* for damages, and force them to part with a good hundred thousand for his trouble.

Zunni's name impressed me; his law firm, on the corner of Caseros and Tacuarí, is one of proverbial sobriety. I inquired whether Zunni had already taken the case. Daneri said he'd be speaking with him that afternoon; then he hesitated, and in that flat, impersonal voice we drop into when we wish to confide something very private, he said he had to have the house so he could finish the poem—because in one corner of the cellar there was an Aleph. He explained that an Aleph is one of the points in space that contain all points.

"It's right under the dining room, in the cellar," he explained. In his distress, his words fairly tumbled out. "*It's mine, it's mine;* I discovered it in my childhood, before I ever attended school. The cellar stairway is steep, and my aunt and uncle had forbidden me to go down it, but somebody said you could go around the world with that thing down there in the basement. The person, whoever it was, was referring, I later learned, to a steamer trunk, but I thought there was some magical contraption down there. I tried to sneak down the stairs, fell head over heels, and when I opened my eyes, I saw the Aleph."

"The Aleph?" I repeated.

"Yes, the place where, without admixture or confusion, all the places of the world, seen from every angle, coexist. I revealed my discovery to no one, but I did return. The child could not understand that he was given that privilege so that the man might carve out a poem! Zunino and Zungri shall never take it from me—never, *never!* Lawbook in hand, Zunni will prove that my Aleph is *inalienable.*"

I tried to think.

"But isn't the cellar quite dark?"

"Truth will not penetrate a recalcitrant understanding. If all the places of the world are within the Aleph, there too will be all stars, all lamps, all sources of light."

"I'll be right over. I want to see it."

I hung up before he could tell me not to come. Sometimes learning a fact is enough to make an entire series of corroborating details, previously unrecognized, fall into place; I was amazed that I hadn't realized until that moment that Carlos Argentino was a madman. All the Viterbos, in fact. . . .Beatriz (I myself have said this many times) was a woman, a girl of implacable clearsightedness, but there were things about her—oversights, distractions, moments of contempt, downright cruelty—that perhaps could have done with a *pathological* explanation. Carlos Argentino's madness filled me with malign happiness; deep down, we had always detested one another.

On Calle Garay, the maid asked me to be so kind as to wait—Sr. Daneri was in the cellar, as he always was, developing photographs. Beside the flowerless vase atop the useless piano smiled the great faded photograph of Beatriz, not so much anachronistic as outside time. No one could see us; in a desperation of tenderness I approached the portrait.

"Beatriz, Beatriz Elena, Beatriz Elena Viterbo," I said. "Belovèd Beatriz, Beatriz lost forever—it's me, it's me, Borges."

Carlos came in shortly afterward. His words were laconic, his tone indifferent; I realized that he was unable to think of anything but the loss of the Aleph.

"A glass of pseudocognac," he said, "and we'll duck right into the cellar. I must forewarn you: dorsal decubitus is essential, as are darkness, immobility, and a certain ocular accommodation. You'll lie on the tile floor and fix your eyes on the nineteenth step of the pertinent stairway. I'll reascend the stairs, let down the trap door, and you'll be alone. Some rodent will frighten you—easy enough to do! Within a few minutes, you will see the Aleph. The microcosm of the alchemists and Kabbalists, our proverbial friend the *multum in parvo*, made flesh!

"Of course," he added, in the dining room, "if you don't see it, that doesn't invalidate anything I've told you. . . .Go on down; within a very short while you will be able to begin a dialogue with *all* the images of Beatriz."

I descended quickly, sick of his vapid chatter. The cellar, barely wider than the stairway, was more like a well or cistern. In vain my eyes sought the trunk that Carlos Argentino had mentioned. A few burlap bags and some crates full of bottles cluttered one corner. Carlos picked up one of the bags, folded it, and laid it out very precisely.

"The couch is a humble one," he explained, "but if I raise it one inch higher, you'll not see a thing, and you'll be cast down and dejected. Stretch that great clumsy body of yours out on the floor and count up nineteen steps."

I followed his ridiculous instructions; he finally left. He carefully let down the trap door; in spite of a chink of light that I began to make out later, the darkness seemed total. Suddenly I realized the danger I was in; I had allowed myself to be locked underground by a madman, after first drinking down a snifter of poison. Carlos' boasting clearly masked the deep-seated fear that I wouldn't see his "miracle"; in order to protect his delirium, in order to hide his madness from himself, *he had to kill me*. I felt a vague discomfort, which I tried to attribute to my rigidity, not to the operation of a narcotic. I closed my eyes, then opened them. It was then that I saw the Aleph.

I come now to the ineffable center of my tale; it is here that a writer's hopelessness begins. Every language is an alphabet of symbols the employment of which assumes a past shared by its interlocutors. How can one transmit to others the infinite Aleph, which my timorous memory can scarcely contain? In a similar situation, mystics have employed a wealth of emblems: to signify the deity, a Persian mystic speaks of a bird that somehow is all birds; Alain de Lille speaks of a sphere whose center is everywhere and circumference nowhere; Ezekiel, of an angel with four faces, facing east and west, north and south at once. (It is not for nothing that I call to mind these inconceivable analogies; they bear a relation to the Aleph.) Perhaps the gods would not deny me the discovery of an equivalent image, but then this report would be polluted with literature, with falseness. And besides, the central problem—the enumeration, even partial enumeration, of infinity—is irresolvable. In that unbounded moment, I saw millions of delightful and horrible acts; none amazed me so much as the fact that all occupied the same point, without superposition and without transparency. What my eyes saw was *simultaneous*; what I shall write is *successive*, because language is successive. Something of it, though, I will capture.

Under the step, toward the right, I saw a small iridescent sphere of almost unbearable brightness. At first I thought it was spinning; then I realized that the movement was an illusion produced by the dizzying spectacles inside it. The Aleph was probably two or three centimeters in diameter, but universal space was contained inside it, with no diminution in size. Each thing (the glass surface of a mirror, let us say) was infinite things, because I could clearly see it from every point in the cosmos. I saw the populous sea, saw dawn and dusk, saw the multitudes of the Americas, saw a silvery spider-web at the center of a black pyramid, saw a broken labyrinth (it was London), saw endless eyes, all very close, studying themselves in me as though in a mirror, saw all the mirrors on the planet (and none of them reflecting me), saw in a rear courtyard on Calle Soler the same tiles I'd seen twenty years before in the entryway of a house in Fray Bentos, saw clusters of grapes, snow, tobacco, veins of metal, water vapor, saw convex equatorial deserts and their every grain of sand, saw a woman in Inverness whom I shall never forget, saw her violent hair, her haughty body, saw a cancer in her breast, saw a circle of dry soil within a sidewalk where there had once been a tree, saw a country house in Adrogué, saw a copy of the first English translation of Pliny (Philemon Holland's), saw every letter of every page at once (as a boy, I would be astounded that the letters in a closed book didn't get all scrambled up together overnight), saw simultaneous night and day, saw a sunset in Querétaro that seemed to reflect the color of a rose in Bengal, saw my bedroom (with no one in it), saw in a study in Alkmaar a globe of the terraqueous world placed between two mirrors that multiplied it endlessly, saw horses with wind-whipped manes on a beach in the Caspian Sea at dawn, saw the delicate bones of a hand, saw the survivors of a battle sending postcards, saw a Tarot card in a shopwindow in Mirzapur, saw the oblique shadows of ferns on the floor of a greenhouse, saw tigers, pistons, bisons, tides, and armies, saw all the ants on earth, saw a Persian astrolabe, saw in a desk drawer (and the handwriting made me tremble) obscene, incredible, detailed letters that Beatriz had sent Carlos Argentino, saw a beloved monument in Chacarita,* saw the horrendous remains of what had once, deliciously, been Beatriz Viterbo, saw the circulation of my dark blood, saw the coils and springs of love and the alterations of death, saw the

Aleph from everywhere at once, saw the earth in the Aleph, and the Aleph once more in the earth and the earth in the Aleph, saw my face and my viscera, saw your face, and I felt dizzy, and I wept, because my eyes had seen that secret, hypothetical object whose name has been usurped by men but which no man has ever truly looked upon: the inconceivable universe.

I had a sense of infinite veneration, infinite pity.

"Serves you right, having your mind boggled, for sticking your nose in where you weren't wanted," said a jovial, bored voice. "And you may rack your brains, but you'll never repay me for this revelation—not in a hundred years. What a magnificent observatory, eh, Borges!"

Carlos Argentino's shoes occupied the highest step. In the sudden half-light, I managed to get to my feet.

"Magnificent . . . Yes, quite . . . magnificent," I stammered.

The indifference in my voice surprised me.

"You did see it?" Carlos Argentino insisted anxiously. "See it clearly? In color and everything?"

Instantly, I conceived my revenge. In the most kindly sort of way—manifestly pitying, nervous, evasive—I thanked Carlos Argentino Daneri for the hospitality of his cellar and urged him to take advantage of the demolition of his house to remove himself from the pernicious influences of the metropolis, which no one— believe me, no one!—can be immune to. I refused, with gentle firmness, to discuss the Aleph; I clasped him by both shoulders as I took my leave and told him again that the country—peace and quiet, you know—was the very best medicine one could take.

Out in the street, on the steps of the Constitución Station, in the subway, all the faces seemed familiar. I feared there was nothing that had the power to surprise or astonish me anymore, I feared that I would never again be without a sense of *déjà vu*. Fortunately, after a few unsleeping nights, forgetfulness began to work in me again.

*

Postscript (March 1, 1943): Six months after the demolition of the building on Calle Garay, Procrustes Publishers, undaunted by the length of Carlos Argentino Daneri's substantial poem, published the first in its series of "Argentine pieces." It goes without saying what happened: Carlos Argentino won second place in the National Prize for Literature.[1] The first prize went to Dr. Aita; third, to Dr. Mario Bonfanti; incredibly, my own work *The Sharper's Cards* did not earn a single vote. Once more, incomprehension and envy triumphed! I have not managed to see Daneri for quite a long time; the newspapers say he'll soon be giving us another volume. His happy pen (belabored no longer by the Aleph) has been consecrated to setting the compendia of Dr. Acevedo Díaz to verse.*

There are two observations that I wish to add: one, with regard to the nature of the Aleph; the other, with respect to its name. Let me begin with the latter: "aleph," as well all know, is the name of the first letter of the alphabet of the sacred language. Its application to the disk of my tale would not appear to be accidental. In the Kabbala, that letter signifies the En Soph, the pure and unlimited godhead; it has also been said that its shape is that of a man pointing to the sky and the earth, to indicate that the lower world is the map and mirror of the higher. For the *Mengenlehre*, the aleph is the symbol of the transfinite numbers, in which the whole is not greater than any of its parts. I would like to know: Did Carlos Argentino choose that name, or did he read it, *applied to another point at which all points converge*, in one of the innumerable texts revealed to him by the Aleph in his house? Incredible as it may seem, I believe that there is (or was) another Aleph; I believe that the Aleph of Calle Garay was a *false* Aleph.

1. "I received your mournful congratulations," he wrote me. "You scoff, my lamentable friend, in envy, but you shall confess—though the words stick in your throat!—that this time I have crowned my cap with the most scarlet of plumes; my turban, with the most caliphal of rubies."

Let me state my reasons. In 1867, Captain Burton was the British consul in Brazil; in July of 1942, Pedro Henríquez Ureña* discovered a manuscript by Burton in a library in Santos, and in this manuscript Burton discussed the mirror attributed in the East to Iskandar dhu-al-Qarnayn, or Alexander the Great of Macedonia. In this glass, Burton said, the entire universe was reflected. Burton mentions other similar artifices—the sevenfold goblet of Kai Khosru; the mirror that Ṭāriq ibn-Ziyād found in a tower (*1001 Nights*, *272*); the mirror that Lucian of Samosata examined on the moon (*True History*, I:26); the specular spear attributed by the first book of Capella's *Satyricon* to Jupiter; Merlin's universal mirror, "round and hollow and . . . [that] seem'd a world of glas" (*Faerie Queene*, III:2, 19)—and then adds these curious words: "But all the foregoing (besides sharing the defect of not existing) are mere optical instruments. The faithful who come to the Amr mosque in Cairo, know very well that the universe lies inside one of the stone columns that surround the central courtyard. . . .No one, of course, can see it, but those who put their ear to the surface claim to hear, within a short time, the bustling rumour of it. . . .The mosque dates to the seventh century; the columns were taken from other, pre-Islamic, temples, for as ibn-Khaldūn has written: *In the republics founded by nomads, the attendance of foreigners is essential for all those things that bear upon masonry*."

Does that Aleph exist, within the heart of a stone? Did I see it when I saw all things, and then forget it? Our minds are permeable to forgetfulness; I myself am distorting and losing, through the tragic erosion of the years, the features of Beatriz.

For Estela Canto

Afterword

Aside from "Emma Zunz" (whose wonderful plot—much superior to its timid execution—was given me by Cecilia Ingenieros) and "Story of the Warrior and the Captive Maiden" (which attempts to interpret two supposedly real occurrences), the stories in this book belong to the genre of fantasy. Of them, the first is the most fully realized; its subject is the effect that immortality would have on humankind. That outline for an ethics of immortality is followed by "The Dead Man"; in that story, Azevedo Bandeira is a man from Rivera or Cerro Largo and also an uncouth sort of deity—a mulatto, renegade version of Chesterton's incomparable Sunday. (Chapter XXIX of *The Decline and Fall of the Roman Empire* tells of a fate much like Otálora's, though considerably grander and more incredible.) About "The Theologians," suffice it to say that they are a dream—a somewhat melancholy dream—of personal identity; about the "Biography of Tadeo Isidoro Cruz," that it is a gloss on the *Martín Fierro*. I owe to a canvas painted by Watts in 1896 the story called "The House of Asterion" and the character of its poor protagonist. "The Other Death" is a fantasy about time, which I wove under the suggestion of some of Pier Damiani's arguments. During the last war, no one could have wished more earnestly than I for Germany's defeat; no one could have felt more strongly than I the tragedy of Germany's fate; "*Deutsches Requiem*" is an attempt to understand that fate, which our own "Germanophiles" (who know nothing of Germany) neither wept over nor even suspected.

"The Writing of the God" has been judged generously; the jaguar obliged me to put into the mouth of a "priest of the Pyramid of Qaholom" the arguments of a Kabbalist or a theologian. In "The Zahir" and "The Aleph," I think I can detect some influence of Wells' story "The Cristal Egg" (1899).

J.L.B.
Buenos Aires,
May 3, 1949

Postscript (1952): I have added four stories to this new edition. "Ibn-Hakam al-Bokhari, Murdered in His Labyrinth" is not (I have been assured) memorable, in spite of its bloodcurdling title. We might think of it as a variation on the story of "The Two Kings in Their Two Labyrinths," interpolated into the *1001 Nights* by the copyists yet passed over by the prudent Galland. About "The Wait" I shall say only that it was suggested by a true police story that Alfredo Doblas read me, some ten years ago, while we were classifying books—following the manual of the Bibliographic Institute of Brussels, I might add, a code I have entirely forgotten save for the detail that God can be found under the number 231. The subject of the story was a Turk; I made him an Italian so that I could more easily get inside his skin. The momentary yet repeated sight of a long, narrow rooming house that sits around the corner of Calle Paraná, in Buenos Aires, provided me with the story titled "The Man on the Threshold"; I set it in India so that its improbability might be bearable.

J.L.B.

The Maker
(1960)

Foreword
For Leopoldo Lugones*

The sounds of the plaza fall behind, and I enter the Library. Almost physically, I can feel the gravitation of the books, the serene atmosphere of orderliness, time magically mounted and preserved. To left and right, absorbed in their waking dream, rows of readers' momentary profiles in the light of the "scholarly lamps," as a Miltonian displacement of adjectives would have it. I recall having recalled that trope here in the Library once before, and then that other adjective of setting—the Lunario's *"arid camel," and then that hexameter from the Æneid that employs, and surpasses, the same artifice:*

Ibant obscuri sola sub nocte per umbram.

These reflections bring me to the door of your office. I go inside. We exchange a few conventional, cordial words, and I give you this book. Unless I am mistaken, you didn't dislike me, Lugones, and you'd have liked to like some work of mine. That never happened, but this time you turn the pages and read a line or two approvingly, perhaps because you've recognized your own voice in it, perhaps because the halting poetry itself is less important than the clean-limbed theory.

At this point, my dream begins to fade and melt away, like water in water. The vast library surrounding me is on Calle México, not Rodríguez Peña, and you, Lugones, killed yourself in early '38. My vanity and my nostalgia have confected a scene that is impossible. Maybe so, I tell myself, but tomorrow I too will be dead and our times will run together and chronology will melt into an orb of symbols, and somehow it will be true to say that I have brought you this book and that you have accepted it.

J.L.B. — Buenos Aires, August 9, 1960

The Maker*

He had never lingered among the pleasures of memory. Impressions, momentary and vivid, would wash over him: a potter's vermilion glaze; the sky-vault filled with stars that were also gods; the moon, from which a lion had fallen; the smoothness of marble under his sensitive, slow fingertips; the taste of wild boar meat, which he liked to tear at with brusque, white bites; a Phoenician word; the black shadow cast by a spear on the yellow sand; the nearness of the sea or women; heavy wine, its harsh edge tempered by honey—these things could flood the entire circuit of his soul. He had known terror, but he had known wrath and courage as well, and once he had been the first to scale an enemy wall. Keen, curious, inadvertent, with no law but satisfaction and immediate indifference, he had wandered the various world and on now this, now that seashore, he had gazed upon the cities of men and their palaces. In teeming marketplaces or at the foot of a mountain upon whose uncertain peak there might be satyrs, he had listened to complex stories, which he took in as he took in reality—without asking whether they were true or false.

Gradually, the splendid universe began drawing away from him; a stubborn fog blurred the lines of his hand; the night lost its peopling stars, the earth became uncertain under his feet. Everything grew distant, and indistinct. When he learned that he was going blind, he cried out. ("Stoicism" had not yet been invented, and Hector could flee without self-diminution.) *Now* (he felt) *I will not be able to see the sky filled with mythological dread or this face that the years will transfigure.* Days and nights passed over this despair of his flesh, but one morning he awoke, looked (with calm now) at the blurred things that lay about him, and felt, inexplicably, the way one might feel upon recognizing a melody or a voice, that all this had happened to him before and that he had faced it with fear but also with joy and hopefulness and curiosity. Then he descended into his memory, which seemed to him endless, and managed to draw up from that vertigo the lost remembrance that gleamed like a coin in the rain—perhaps because he had never really looked at it except (perhaps) in a dream.

The memory was this: Another boy had insulted him, and he had run to his father and told him the story. As though he weren't paying attention, or didn't understand, his father let him talk, but then he took a bronze knife down from the wall—a beautiful knife, charged with power, that the boy had furtively coveted. Now he held it in his hands, and the surprise of possession wiped away the insult that he had suffered, but his father's voice was speaking: *Let it be known that you are a man*, and there was a command in the voice. Night's blindness was upon the paths; clutching to himself the knife in which he sensed a magical power, the boy descended the steep rough hillside that his house stood on and ran to the seashore, dreaming that he was Ajax and Perseus and peopling the dark salt air with wounds and battles. It was the precise flavor of that moment that he sought for now; the rest didn't matter—the insulting words of his challenge, the clumsy combat, the return with the bloodied blade.

Another memory, in which there was also a night and the foretaste of adventure, sprouted from that first one. A woman, the first woman the gods had given him, had awaited him in the darkness of a subterranean crypt, and he searched for her through galleries that were like labyrinths of stone and down slopes that descended into darkness. Why had those memories come to him, and why did they come without bitterness, like some mere foreshadowing of the present?

With grave wonder, he understood. In this night of his mortal eyes into which he was descending, love and adventure were also awaiting him. Ares and Aphrodite—because now he began to sense (because now he began to be surrounded by) a rumor of glory and hexameters, a rumor of men who defend a temple that the gods will not save, a rumor of black ships that set sail in search of a beloved isle, the rumor of the *Odysseys* and *Iliads* that it was his fate to sing and to leave echoing in the cupped hands of human memory. These things we know, but not those that he felt as he descended into his last darkness.

Dreamtigers*

In my childhood I was a fervent worshiper of the tiger—not the jaguar, that spotted "tiger"* that inhabits the floating islands of water hyacinths along the Paraná and the tangled wilderness of the Amazon, but the true tiger, the striped Asian breed that can be faced only by men of war, in a castle atop an elephant. I would stand for hours on end before one of the cages at the zoo; I would rank vast encyclopedias and natural history books by the splendor of their tigers. (I still remember those pictures, I who cannot recall without error a woman's brow or smile.) My childhood outgrown, the tigers and my passion for them faded, but they are still in my dreams. In that underground sea or chaos, they still endure. As I sleep I am drawn into some dream or other, and suddenly I realize that it's a dream. At those moments, I often think: *This is a dream, a pure diversion of my will, and since I have unlimited power, I am going to bring forth a tiger.*

Oh, incompetence! My dreams never seem to engender the creature I so hunger for. The tiger does appear, but it is all dried up, or it's flimsy-looking, or it has impure vagaries of shape or an unacceptable size, or it's altogether too ephemeral, or it looks more like a dog or bird than like a tiger.

A Dialog About a Dialog

A: Absorbed in our discussion of immortality, we had let night fall without lighting the lamp, and we couldn't see each other's faces. With an off-handedness or gentleness more convincing than passion would have been, Macedonio Fernández' voice said once more that the soul is immortal. He assured me that the death of the body is altogether insignificant, and that dying has to be the most unimportant thing that can happen to a man. I was playing with Macedonio's pocketknife, opening and closing it. A nearby accordion was infinitely dispatching *La Comparsita*, that dismaying trifle that so many people like because it's been misrepresented to them as being old. . . .I suggested to Macedonio that we kill ourselves, so we might have our discussion without all that racket.
Z: (mockingly) But I suspect that at the last moment you reconsidered.
A: (now deep in mysticism) Quite frankly, I don't remember whether we committed suicide that night or not.

Toenails

Gentle socks pamper them by day, and shoes cobbled of leather fortify them, but my toes hardly notice. All they're interested in is turning out toenails—semitransparent, flexible sheets of a hornlike material, as defense against—*whom*? Brutish, distrustful as only they can be, my toes labor ceaselessly at manufacturing that frail armament. They turn their backs on the universe and its ecstasies in order to spin out, endlessly, those ten pointless projectile heads, which are cut away time and again by the sudden snips of a Solingen. By the ninetieth twilit day of their prenatal confinement, my toes had cranked up that extraordinary factory. And when I am tucked away in Recoleta,* in an ash-colored house bedecked with dry flowers and amulets, they will still be at their stubborn work, until corruption at last slows them—them and the beard upon my cheeks.

Covered Mirrors

Islam tells us that on the unappealable Day of Judgment, all who have perpetrated images of living things will reawaken with their works, and will be ordered to blow life into them, and they will fail, and they and their works will be cast into the fires of punishment. As a child, I knew that horror of the spectral duplication or multiplication of reality, but mine would come as I stood before large mirrors. As soon as it began to grow dark outside, the constant, infallible functioning of mirrors, the way they followed my every movement, their cosmic pantomime, would seem eerie to me. One of my insistent pleas to God and my guardian angel was that I not dream of mirrors; I recall clearly that I would keep one eye on them uneasily. I feared sometimes that they would begin to veer off from reality; other times, that I would see my face in them disfigured by strange misfortunes. I have learned that this horror is monstrously abroad in the world again. The story is quite simple, and terribly unpleasant.

In 1927, I met a grave young woman, first by telephone (because Julia began as a voice without a name or face) and then on a corner at nightfall. Her eyes were alarmingly large, her hair jet black and straight, her figure severe. She was the granddaughter and great-granddaughter of Federalists, as I was the grandson and great-grandson of Unitarians,* but that ancient discord between our lineages was, for us, a bond, a fuller possession of our homeland. She lived with her family in a big run-down high-ceiling'd house, in the resentment and savorlessness of genteel poverty. In the afternoons—only very rarely at night—we would go out walking through her neighborhood, which was Balvanera.* We would stroll along beside the high blank wall of the railway yard; once we walked down Sarmiento all the way to the cleared grounds of the Parque Centenario.* Between us there was neither love itself nor the fiction of love; I sensed in her an intensity that was utterly unlike the intensity of eroticism, and I feared it. In order to forge an intimacy with women, one often tells them about true or apocryphal things that happened in one's youth; I must have told her at some point about my horror of mirrors, and so in 1928 I must have planted the hallucination that was to flower in 1931. Now I have just learned that she has gone insane, and that in her room all the mirrors are covered, because she sees my reflection in them—usurping her own—and she trembles and cannot speak, and says that I am magically following her, watching her, stalking her.

What dreadful bondage, the bondage of my face—or one of my former faces. Its odious fate makes *me* odious as well, but I don't care anymore.

Argumentum Ornithologicum

I close my eyes and see a flock of birds. The vision lasts a second, or perhaps less; I am not sure how many birds I saw. Was the number of birds definite or indefinite? The problem involves the existence of God. If God exists, the number is definite, because God knows how many birds I saw. If God does not exist, the number is indefinite, because no one can have counted. In this case I saw fewer than ten birds (let us say) and more than one, but did not see nine, eight, seven, six, five, four, three, or two birds. I saw a number between ten and one, which was not nine, eight, seven, six, five, etc. That integer—not-nine, not-eight, not-seven, not-six, not-five, etc.—is inconceivable. *Ergo*, God exists.

The Captive

In Junín or Tapalquén, they tell the story. A young boy disappeared in an Indian raid; people said the Indians had kidnapped him. His parents searched for him without success. Many years went by, and a soldier coming into town from the interior told them about an Indian with sky blue eyes who might well be their son. They finally managed to find this Indian (the story has lost many of its details, and I don't want to invent what I don't know) and thought they recognized him. Shaped by the wilderness and his barbaric life, the man could no longer understand the words of his mother tongue, but he allowed himself to be led—indifferently, docilely—back to the house. There, he stopped (perhaps because the others stopped). He looked at the door, almost uncomprehendingly. Then suddenly he bowed his head, gave an odd cry, rushed down the entryway and through the two long patios, and ran into the kitchen. He thrust his arm unhesitatingly up into the blackened chimney of the stove and took out the little horn-handled knife he had hidden there when he was a boy. His eyes gleamed with happiness and his parents wept, because they had found their son.

That memory may have been followed by others, but the Indian could not live a life that was hemmed about by walls, and one day he went off in search of his wilderness. I would like to know what he felt in that moment of vertigo when past and present intermingled; I would like to know whether the lost son was reborn and died in that ecstatic moment, and whether he ever managed to recognize, even as little as a baby or a dog might, his parents and the house.

The Mountebank

One day in July, 1952, the man dressed in mourning weeds appeared in that little village on the Chaco River.* He was a tall, thin man with vaguely Indian features and the inexpressive face of a half-wit or a mask. The townsfolk treated him with some deference, not because of who he was but because of the personage he was portraying or had by now become. He chose a house near the river; with the help of some neighbor women he laid a board across two sawhorses, and on it he set a pasteboard coffin with a blond-haired mannequin inside. In addition, they lighted four candles in tall candleholders and put flowers all around. The townsfolk soon began to gather. Old ladies bereft of hope, dumbstruck wide-eyed boys, peons who respectfully took off their pith hats—they filed past the coffin and said: *My condolences, General.* The man in mourning sat sorrowfully at the head of the coffin, his hands crossed over his belly like a pregnant woman. He would extend his right hand to shake the hand extended to him and answer with courage and resignation: *It was fate. Everything humanly possible was done.* A tin collection box received the two-peso price of admission, and many could not content themselves with a single visit.

What kind of man, I ask myself, thought up and then acted out that funereal farce—a fanatic? a grief-stricken mourner? a madman? a cynical impostor? Did he, in acting out his mournful role as the macabre widower, believe himself to be Perón? It is an incredible story, but it actually happened—and perhaps not once but many times, with different actors and local variants. In it, one can see the perfect symbol of an unreal time, and it is like the reflection of a dream or like that play within a play in *Hamlet*. The man in mourning was not Perón and the blond-haired mannequin was not the woman Eva Duarte, but then Perón was not Perón, either, nor was Eva, Eva—they were unknown or anonymous persons (whose secret name and true face we shall never know) who acted out, for the credulous love of the working class, a crass and ignoble mythology.

Delia Elena San Marco

We said good-bye on one of the corners of the Plaza del Once.*

From the sidewalk on the other side of the street I turned and looked back; you had turned, and you waved good-bye.

A river of vehicles and people ran between us; it was five o'clock on no particular afternoon. How was I to know that that river was the sad Acheron, which no one may cross twice?

Then we lost sight of each other, and a year later you were dead.

And now I search out that memory and gaze at it and think that it was false, that under the trivial farewell there lay an infinite separation.

Last night I did not go out after dinner. To try to understand these things, I reread the last lesson that Plato put in his teacher's mouth. I read that the soul can flee when the flesh dies.

And now I am not sure whether the truth lies in the ominous later interpretation or in the innocent farewell.

Because if the soul doesn't die, we are right to lay no stress on our good-byes.

To say good-bye is to deny separation; it is to say *Today we play at going our own ways, but we'll see each other tomorrow.* Men invented farewells because they somehow knew themselves to be immortal, even while seeing themselves as contingent and ephemeral.

One day we will pick up this uncertain conversation again, Delia—on the bank of what river?—and we will ask ourselves whether we were once, in a city that vanished into the plains, Borges and Delia.

A Dialog Between Dead Men

The man arrived from the south of England early one winter morning in 1877. As he was a ruddy, athletic, overweight man, it was inevitable that almost everyone should think that he was English, and indeed he looked remarkably like the archetypical John Bull. He wore a bowler hat and a curious wool cape with an opening in the center. A group of men, women, and babes were waiting for him anxiously; many of them had a red line scored across their throats, others were headless and walked with hesitant, fearful steps, as though groping through the dark. Little by little, they encircled the stranger, and from the back of the crowd someone shouted out a curse, but an ancient terror stopped them, and they dared go no further. From out of their midst stepped a sallow-skinned soldier with eyes like glowing coals; his long tangled hair and lugubrious beard seemed to consume his face; ten or twelve mortal wounds furrowed his body, like the stripes on a tiger's skin. When the newcomer saw him, he paled, but then he stepped forward and put out his hand.

"How grievous it is to see such a distinguished soldier brought low by the instruments of perfidy!" he said, grandiloquently. "And yet what deep satisfaction to have ordered that the torturers and assassins atone for their crimes on the scaffold in the Plaza de la Victoria!"

"If it's Santos Pérez and the Reinafé brothers you're referring to, be assured that I have already thanked them,"' the bloody man said with slow solemnity.

The other man looked at him as though smelling a gibe or a threat, but Quiroga* went on:

"You never understood me, Rosas.* But how could you understand me, if our lives were so utterly different? Your fate was to govern in a city that looks out toward Europe and that one day will be one of the most famous cities in the world; mine was to wage war across the solitudes of the Americas, in an impoverished land inhabited by impoverished gauchos. My empire was one of spears and shouts and sandy wastelands and virtually secret victories in godforsaken places. What sort of claim to fame is that? I live in people's memory—and will go on living there for many years—because I was murdered in a stagecoach in a place called Barranca Yaco by a gang of men with swords and horses. I owe to you that gift of a valiant death, which I cannot say I was grateful for at the time but which subsequent generations have been loath to forget. You are surely familiar with certain primitive lithographs and that interesting literary work penned by a worthy from San Juan?"

Rosas, who had recovered his composure, looked at the other man contemptuously.

"You are a romantic," he said with a sneer. "The flattery of posterity is worth very little more than the flattery of one's contemporaries, which is not worth anything, and can be bought with a pocketful of loose change."

"I know how you think," replied Quiroga. "In 1852, fate, which is generous, or which wanted to plumb you to the very depths, offered you a man's death, in battle. You showed yourself unworthy of that gift, because fighting, bloodshed, frightened you."

"Frightened me?" Rosas repeated. "Me, who've tamed horses in the South and then tamed an entire country?"

For the first time, Quiroga smiled.

"I know," he slowly said, "from the impartial testimony of your peons and seconds-in-command, that you did more than one pretty turn on horseback, but back in those days, across the Americas—and on horseback, too—other pretty turns were done in places named Chacabuco and Junín and Palma Redondo and Caseros."*

Rosas listened expressionlessly, and then replied.

' "I had no need to be brave. One of those pretty turns of mine, as you put it, was to manage to convince braver men than I to fight and die for me. Santos Pérez, for example, who was more than a match for *you*. Bravery is a matter of bearing up; some men bear up better than others, but sooner or later, every man caves in."

"That may be," Quiroga said, "but I have lived and I have died, and to this day I don't know what fear is. And now I am going to the place where I will be given a new face and a new destiny, because history is tired of violent men. I don't know who the next man may be, what will be done with me, but I know I won't be afraid."

"I'm content to be who I am," said Rosas, "and I have no wish to be anybody else."

"Stones want to go on being stones, too, forever and ever," Quiroga replied. "And for centuries they are stones—until they crumble into dust. When I first entered into death, I thought the way you do, but I've learned many things here since. If you notice, we're both already changing."

But Rosas paid him no attention; he merely went on, as though thinking out loud:

"Maybe I'm not cut out to be dead, but this place and this conversation seem like a dream to me, and not a dream that *I* am dreaming, either. More like a dream dreamed by somebody else, somebody that's not born yet."

Then their conversation ended, because just then Someone called them.

The Plot

To make his horror perfect, Cæsar, hemmed about at the foot of a statue by his friends' impatient knives, discovers among the faces and the blades the face of Marcus Junius Brutus, his ward, perhaps his very son—and so Cæsar stops defending himself, and cries out *Et tu, Brute?* Shakespeare and Quevedo record that pathetic cry.

Fate is partial to repetitions, variations, symmetries. Nineteen centuries later, in the southern part of the province of Buenos Aires, a gaucho is set upon by other gauchos, and as he falls he recognizes a godson of his, and says to him in gentle remonstrance and slow surprise (these words must be heard, not read): *Pero, iché!* He dies, but he does not know that he has died so that a scene can be played out again.

A Problem

Let us imagine that a piece of paper with a text in Arabic on it is discovered in Toledo, and that paleographers declare the text to have been written by that same Cide Hamete Benengeli from whom Cervantes derived *Don Quixote*. In it, we read that the hero (who, as everyone knows, wandered the roads of Spain armed with a lance and sword, challenging anyone for any reason) discovers, after one of his many combats, that he has killed a man. At that point the fragment breaks off; the problem is to guess, or hypothesize, how don Quixote reacts.

So far as I can see, there are three possibilities. The first is a negative one: Nothing in particular happens, because in the hallucinatory world of don Quixote, death is no more uncommon than magic, and there is no reason that killing a mere man should disturb one who does battle, or thinks he does battle, with fabled beasts and sorcerers. The second is pathetic: Don Quixote never truly managed to forget that he was a creation, a projection, of Alonso Quijano, reader of fabulous tales. The sight of death, the realization that a delusion has led him to commit the sin of Cain, awakens him from his willful madness, perhaps forever. The third is perhaps the most plausible: Having killed the man, don Quixote cannot allow himself to think that the terrible act is the work of a delirium; the reality of the effect makes him assume a like reality of cause, and don Quixote never emerges from his madness.

But there is yet another hypothesis, which is alien to the Spanish mind (even to the Western mind) and which requires a more ancient, more complex, and more timeworn setting. Don Quixote—who is no longer don Quixote but a king of the cycles of Hindustan—senses, as he stands before the body of his enemy, that killing and engendering are acts of God or of magic, which everyone knows transcend the human condition. He knows that death is illusory, as are the bloody sword that lies heavy in his hand, he himself and his entire past life, and the vast gods and the universe.

The Yellow Rose

It was neither that afternoon nor the next that Giambattista Marino died—that illustrious man proclaimed by the unanimous mouths of Fame (to use an image that was dear to him) as the new Homer or the new Dante—and yet the motionless and silent act that took place that afternoon was, in fact, the last thing that happened in his life. His brow laureled with years and glory, the man died in a vast Spanish bed with carven pillars. It costs us nothing to picture a serene balcony a few steps away, looking out toward the west, and, below, marbles and laurels and a garden whose terraced steps are mirrored in a rectangular pool. In a goblet, a woman has set a yellow rose; the man murmurs the inevitable lines of poetry that even he, to tell the truth, is a bit tired of by now:

> Porpora de' giardin, pompa de' prato,
> Gemma di primavera, occhio d'aprile . . .*

Then the revelation occurred. Marino *saw* the rose, as Adam had seen it in Paradise, and he realized that it lay within its own eternity, not within his words, and that we might speak about the rose, allude to it, but never truly express it, and that the tall, haughty volumes that made a golden dimness in the corner of his room were not (as his vanity had dreamed them) a mirror of the world, but just another thing added to the world's contents.

Marino achieved that epiphany on the eve of his death, and Homer and Dante may have achieved it as well.

The Witness

In a stable that stands almost in the shadow of the new stone church, a man with gray eyes and gray beard, lying amid the odor of the animals, humbly tries to will himself into death, much as a man might will himself to sleep. The day, obedient to vast and secret laws, slowly shifts about and mingles the shadows in the lowly place; outside lie plowed fields, a ditch clogged with dead leaves, and the faint track of a wolf in the black clay where the line of woods begins. The man sleeps and dreams, forgotten. The bells for orisons awaken him. Bells are now one of evening's customs in the kingdoms of England, but as a boy the man has seen the face of Woden, the sacred horror and the exultation, the clumsy wooden idol laden with Roman coins and ponderous vestments, the sacrifice of horses, dogs, and prisoners. Before dawn he will be dead, and with him, the last eyewitness images of pagan rites will perish, never to be seen again. The world will be a little poorer when this Saxon man is dead.

Things, events, that occupy space yet come to an end when someone dies may make us stop in wonder—and yet one thing, or an infinite number of things, dies with every man's or woman's death, unless the universe itself has a memory, as theosophists have suggested. In the course of time there was one day that closed the last eyes that had looked on Christ; the Battle of Junín and the love of Helen died with the death of one man. What will die with me the day I die? What pathetic or frail image will be lost to the world? The voice of Macedonio Fernán-

dez, the image of a bay horse in a vacant lot on the corner of
Sarrano and Charcas, a bar of sulfur in the drawer of a mahogany
desk?

Martín Fierro

Out of this city marched armies that seemed grand, and that in later days *were* grand, thanks to the magnifying effects of glory. After many years, one of the soldiers returned, and in a foreign accent told stories of what had happened to him in places called Ituzaingó or Ayacucho.* These things are now as though they had never been.

There have been two tyrannies in this land. During the first, a wagon pulled out of La Plata market; as the wagon passed through the streets, some men on the driver's seat cried out their wares, hawking white and yellow peaches; a young boy lifted the corner of the canvas that covered them and saw the heads of Unitarians, their beards bloody.* The second meant, for many, prison and death; for all, it meant discomfort, endless humiliation, a taste of shamefulness in the actions of every day. These things are now as though they had never been.

A man who knew all the words looked with painstaking love at the plants and birds of this land and defined them, perhaps forever, and in metaphors of metal wrote the vast chronicle of its tumultuous sunsets and the shapes of its moon.* These things are now as though they had never been.

Also in this land have generations known those common yet somehow eternal vicissitudes that are the stuff of art. These things are now as though they had never been, but in a hotel room in eighteen-hundred sixty-something a man dreamed of a knife fight. A gaucho lifts a black man off the ground with the thrust of his knife, drops him like a bag of bones, watches him writhe in pain and die, squats down to wipe off his knife, unties his horse's bridle and swings up into the saddle slowly, so no one will think he's running away from what he's done. This thing that was once, returns again, infinitely; the visible armies have gone and what is left is a common sort of knife fight; one man's dream is part of all men's memory.

Mutations

In a hallway I saw a sign with an arrow pointing the way, and I was struck by the thought that that inoffensive symbol had once been a thing of iron, an inexorable, mortal projectile that had penetrated the flesh of men and lions and clouded the sun of Thermopylæ and bequeathed to Harald Sigurdson, for all time, six feet of English earth.

Several days later, someone showed me a photograph of a Magyar horseman; a coil of rope hung about his mount's chest. I learned that the rope, which had once flown through the air and lassoed bulls in the pasture, was now just an insolent decoration on a rider's Sunday riding gear.

In the cemetery on the Westside I saw a runic cross carved out of red marble; its arms splayed and widened toward the ends and it was bounded by a circle. That circumscribed and limited cross was a figure of the cross with unbound arms that is in turn the symbol of the gallows on which a god was tortured—that "vile machine" decried by Lucian of Samosata.

Cross, rope, and arrow: ancient implements of mankind, today reduced, or elevated, to symbols. I do not know why I marvel at them so, when there is nothing on earth that forgetfulness does not fade, memory alter, and when no one knows what sort of image the future may translate it into.

Parable of Cervantes and the Quixote

Weary of his land of Spain, an old soldier of the king's army sought solace in the vast geographies of Ariosto, in that valley of the moon in which one finds the time that is squandered by dreams, and in the golden idol of Muhammad stolen by Montalbán.

In gentle self-mockery, this old soldier conceived a credulous man—his mind unsettled by the reading of all those wonders—who took it into his head to ride out in search of adventures and enchantments in prosaic places with names such as El Toboso and Montiel.

Defeated by reality, by Spain, don Quixote died in 1614 in the town of his birth. He was survived only a short time by Miguel de Cervantes.

For both the dreamer and the dreamed, that entire adventure had been the clash of two worlds; the unreal world of romances and the common everyday world of the seventeenth century.

They never suspected that the years would at last smooth away the discord, never suspected that in the eyes of the future, La Mancha and Montiel and the lean figure of the Knight of Mournful Countenance would be no less poetic than the adventures of Sindbad or the vast geographies of Ariosto.

For in the beginning of literature there is myth, as there is also in the end of it.

Devoto Clinic
January 1955

Paradiso, *XXXI*, *108*

Diodorus Siculus tells the story of a god that is cut into pieces and scattered over the earth. Which of us, walking through the twilight or retracing some day in our past, has never felt that we have lost some infinite thing?

Mankind has lost a face, an irrecoverable face, and all men wish they could be that pilgrim (dreamed in the empyrean, under the Rose) who goes to Rome and looks upon the veil of St. Veronica and murmurs in belief: *My Lord Jesus Christ, very God, is this, indeed, Thy likeness in such fashion wrought?**

There is a face in stone beside a path, and an inscription that reads *The True Portrait of the Holy Face of the Christ of Jaén*. If we really knew what that face looked like, we would possess the key to the parables, and know whether the son of the carpenter was also the Son of God.

Paul saw the face as a light that struck him to the ground; John, as the sun when it shines forth in all its strength; Teresa de Jesús, many times, bathed in serene light, although she could never say with certainty what the color of its eyes was.

Those features are lost to us, as a magical number created from our customary digits can be lost, as the image in a kaleidoscope is lost forever. We can see them and yet not *grasp* them. A Jew's profile in the subway might be the profile of Christ; the hands that give us back change at a ticket booth may mirror those that soldiers nailed one day to the cross.

Some feature of the crucified face may lurk in every mirror;

perhaps the face died, faded away, so that God might be all faces.

Who knows but that tonight we may see it in the labyrinths of dream, and not know tomorrow that we saw it.

Parable of the Palace

That day the Yellow Emperor showed his palace to the poet. Little by little, step by step, they left behind, in long procession, the first westward-facing terraces which, like the jagged hemicycles of an almost unbounded amphitheater, stepped down into a paradise, a garden whose metal mirrors and intertwined hedges of juniper were a prefiguration of the labyrinth. Cheerfully they lost themselves in it—at first as though condescending to a game, but then not without some uneasiness, because its straight *allées* suffered from a very gentle but continuous curvature, so that secretly the avenues were circles. Around midnight, observation of the planets and the opportune sacrifice of a tortoise allowed them to escape the bonds of that region that seemed enchanted, though not to free themselves from that sense of being lost that accompanied them to the end. They wandered next through antechambers and courtyards and libraries, and then through a hexagonal room with a water clock, and one morning, from a tower, they made out a man of stone, whom later they lost sight of forever. In canoes hewn from sandalwood, they crossed many gleaming rivers—or perhaps a single river many times. The imperial entourage would pass and people would fall to their knees and bow their heads to the ground, but one day the courtiers came to an island where one man did not do this, for he had never seen the Celestial Son before, and the executioner had to decapitate him. The eyes of the emperor and poet looked with indifference on black tresses and black dances and golden masks; the real merged and mingled with the dreamed—or the real, rather, was one of the shapes the dream took. It seemed impossible that the earth should be anything but gardens, fountains, architectures, and forms of splendor. Every hundred steps a tower cut the air; to the eye, their color was identical, but the first of them was yellow and the last was scarlet; that was how delicate the gradations were and how long the series.

It was at the foot of the penultimate tower that the poet (who had appeared untouched by the spectacles which all the others had so greatly marveled at) recited the brief composition that we link indissolubly to his name today, the words which, as the most elegant historians never cease repeating, garnered the poet immortality and death. The text has been lost; there are those who believe that it consisted of but a single line; others, of a single word.

What we do know—however incredible it may be—is that within the poem lay the entire enormous palace, whole and to the least detail, with every venerable porcelain it contained and every scene on every porcelain, all the lights and shadows of its twilights, and every forlorn or happy moment of the glorious dynasties of mortals, gods, and dragons that had lived within it through all its endless past. Everyone fell silent; then the emperor spoke. "You have stolen my palace!" he cried, and the executioner's iron scythe mowed down the poet's life.

Others tell the story differently. The world cannot contain two things that are identical; no sooner, they say, had the poet uttered his poem than the palace disappeared, as though in a puff of smoke, wiped from the face of the earth by the final syllable.

Such legends, of course, are simply literary fictions. The poet was the emperor's slave and died a slave; his composition fell into oblivion because it merited oblivion, and his descendants still seek, though they shall never find, the word for the universe.

Everything and Nothing*

There was no one inside him; behind his face (which even in the bad paintings of the time resembles no other) and his words (which were multitudinous, and of a fantastical and agitated turn) there was no more than a slight chill, a dream someone had failed to dream. At first he thought that everyone was like him, but the surprise and bewilderment of an acquaintance to whom he began to describe that hollowness showed him his error, and also let him know, forever after, that an individual ought not to differ from its species. He thought at one point that books might hold some remedy for his condition, and so he learned the "little Latin and less Greek" that a contemporary would later mention. Then he reflected that what he was looking for might be found in the performance of an elemental ritual of humanity, and so he allowed himself to be initiated by Anne Hathaway one long evening in June.

At twenty-something he went off to London. Instinctively, he had already trained himself to the habit of feigning that he was somebody, so that his "nobodiness" might not be discovered. In London he found the calling he had been predestined to; he became an actor, that person who stands upon a stage and plays at being another person, for an audience of people who play at taking him for that person. The work of a thespian held out a remarkable happiness to him—the first, perhaps, he had ever known; but when the last line was delivered and the last dead man applauded off the stage, the hated taste of unreality would assail him. He would cease being Ferrex or Tamerlane and return to being nobody. Haunted, hounded, he began imagining other heroes, other tragic fables. Thus while his body, in whorehouses and taverns around London, lived its life as body, the soul that lived inside it would be Cæsar, who ignores the admonition of the sibyl, and Juliet, who hates the lark, and Macbeth, who speaks on the moor with the witches who are also the Fates, the Three Weird Sisters. No one was as many men as that man—that man whose repertoire, like that of the Egyptian Proteus, was all the appearances of being. From time to time he would leave a confession in one corner or another of the work, certain that it would not be deciphered; Richard says that inside himself, he plays the part of many, and Iago says, with curious words, *I am not what I am*. The fundamental identity of living, dreaming, and performing inspired him to famous passages.

For twenty years he inhabited that guided and directed hallucination, but one morning he was overwhelmed with the surfeit and horror of being, so many kings that die by the sword and so many unrequited lovers who come together, separate, and melodiously expire. That very day, he decided to sell his theater. Within a week he had returned to his birthplace, where he recovered the trees and the river of his childhood and did not associate them with those others, fabled with mythological allusion and Latin words, that his muse had celebrated. He had to be somebody; he became a retired businessman who'd made a fortune and had an interest in loans, lawsuits, and petty usury. It was in that role that he dictated the arid last will and testament that we know today, from which he deliberately banished every trace of sentiment or literature. Friends from London would visit his retreat, and he would once again play the role of poet for them.

History adds that before or after he died, he discovered himself standing before God, and said to Him: *I, who have been so many men in vain, wish to be one, to be myself.* God's voice answered him out of a whirlwind: *I, too, am not I; I dreamed the world as you, Shakespeare, dreamed your own work, and among the forms of my dream are you, who like me are many, yet no one.*

Ragnarök

The images in dreams, wrote Coleridge, figure forth the impressions that our intellect would call causes; we do not feel horror because we are haunted by a sphinx, we dream a sphinx in order to explain the horror that we feel. If that is true, how might a mere chronicling of its forms transmit the stupor, the exultation, the alarms, the dread, and the joy that wove together that night's dream? I shall attempt that chronicle, nonetheless; perhaps the fact that the dream consisted of but a single scene may erase or soften the essential difficulty.

The place was the College of Philosophy and Letters; the hour, nightfall. Everything (as is often the case in dreams) was slightly different; a slight magnification altered things. We chose authorities; I would speak with Pedro Henríquez Ureña,* who in waking life had died many years before. Suddenly, we were dumbfounded by a great noise of demonstrators or street musicians. From the Underworld, we heard the cries of humans and animals. A voice cried: *Here they come!* and then: *The gods! the gods!* Four or five individuals emerged from out of the mob and occupied the dais of the auditorium. Everyone applauded, weeping; it was the gods, returning after a banishment of many centuries. Looming larger than life as they stood upon the dais, their heads thrown back and their chests thrust forward, they haughtily received our homage. One of them was holding a branch (which belonged, no doubt, to the simple botany of dreams); another, with a sweeping gesture, held out a hand that was a claw; one of Janus' faces looked mistrustfully at Thoth's curved beak. Perhaps excited by our applause, one of them, I no longer remember which, burst out in a triumphant, incredibly bitter clucking that was half gargle and half whistle. From that point on, things changed.

It all began with the suspicion (perhaps exaggerated) that the gods were unable to talk. Centuries of a feral life of flight had atrophied that part of them that was human; the moon of Islam and the cross of Rome had been implacable with these fugitives. Beetling brows, yellowed teeth, the sparse beard of a mulatto or a Chinaman, and beastlike dewlaps were testaments to the degeneration of the Olympian line. The clothes they wore were not those of a decorous and honest poverty, but rather of the criminal luxury of the Underworld's gambling dens and houses of ill repute. A carnation bled from a buttonhole; under a tight suitcoat one could discern the outline of a knife. Suddenly, we felt that they were playing their last trump, that they were cunning, ignorant, and cruel, like aged predators, and that if we allowed ourselves to be swayed by fear or pity, they would wind up destroying us.

We drew our heavy revolvers (suddenly in the dream there were revolvers) and exultantly killed the gods.

Inferno, *I, 32*

From the half-light of dawn to the half-light of evening, the eyes of a leopard, in the last years of the twelfth century, looked upon a few wooden boards, some vertical iron bars, some varying men and women, a blank wall, and perhaps a stone gutter littered with dry leaves. The leopard did not know, could not know, that it yearned for love and cruelty and the hot pleasure of tearing flesh and a breeze with the scent of deer, but something inside it was suffocating and howling in rebellion, and God spoke to it in a dream: *You shall live and die in this prison, so that a man that I have knowledge of may see you a certain number of times and never forget you and put your figure and your symbol into a poem, which has its exact place in the weft of the universe. You suffer captivity, but you shall have given a word to the poem.* In the dream, God illuminated the animal's rude understanding and the animal grasped the reasons and accepted its fate, but when it awoke there was only an obscure resignation in it, a powerful ignorance, because the machine of the world is exceedingly complex for the simplicity of a savage beast.

Years later, Dante was to die in Ravenna, as unjustified and alone as any other man. In a dream, God told him the secret purpose of his life and work; Dante, astonished, learned at last who he was and what he was, and he blessed the bitternesses of his life. Legend has it that when he awoke, he sensed that he had received and lost an infinite thing, something he would never be able to recover, or even to descry from afar, because the machine of the world is exceedingly complex for the simplicity of men.

Borges and I

It's Borges, the other one, that things happen to. I walk through Buenos Aires and I pause—mechanically now, perhaps—to gaze at the arch of an entryway and its inner door; news of Borges reaches me by mail, or I see his name on a list of academics or in some biographical dictionary. My taste runs to hourglasses, maps, eighteenth-century typefaces, etymologies, the taste of coffee, and the prose of Robert Louis Stevenson; Borges shares those preferences, but in a vain sort of way that turns them into the accoutrements of an actor. It would be an exaggeration to say that our relationship is hostile—I live, I allow myself to live, so that Borges can spin out his literature, and that literature is my justification. I willingly admit that he has written a number of sound pages, but those pages will not save *me*, perhaps because the good in them no longer belongs to any individual, not even to that other man, but rather to language itself, or to tradition. Beyond that, I am doomed—utterly and inevitably—to oblivion, and fleeting moments will be all of me that survives in that other man. Little by little, I have been turning everything over to him, though I know the perverse way he has of distorting and magnifying everything. Spinoza believed that all things wish to go on being what they are—stone wishes eternally to be stone, and tiger, to be tiger. I shall endure in Borges, not in myself (if, indeed, I am anybody at all), but I recognize myself less in his books than in many others', or in the tedious strumming of a guitar. Years ago I tried to free myself from him, and I moved on from the mythologies of the slums and outskirts of the city to games with time and infinity, but those games belong to Borges now, and I shall have to think up other things. So my life is a point-counterpoint, a kind of fugue, and a falling away—and everything winds up being lost to me, and everything falls into oblivion, or into the hands of the other man.

I am not sure which of us it is that's writing this page.

Museum

On Exactitude in Science

. . . In that Empire, the Art of Cartography attained such Perfection that the map of a single Province occupied the entirety of a City, and the map of the Empire, the entirety of a Province. In time, those Unconscionable Maps no longer satisfied, and the Cartographers Guilds struck a Map of the Empire whose size was that of the Empire, and which coincided point for point with it. The following Generations, who were not so fond of the Study of Cartography as their Forebears had been, saw that that vast Map was Useless, and not without some Pitilessness was it, that they delivered it up to the Inclemencies of Sun and Winters. In the Deserts of the West, still today, there are Tattered Ruins of that Map, inhabited by Animals and Beggars; in all the Land there is no other Relic of the Disciplines of Geography.

Suárez Miranda, *Viajes de varones prudentes*,
Libro IV, Cap. XLV, Lérida, 1658

In Memoriam, J.F.K.

This bullet is an old one.

In 1897, it was fired at the president of Uruguay by a young man from Montevideo, Avelino Arredondo,* who had spent long weeks without seeing anyone so that the world might know that he acted alone. Thirty years earlier, Lincoln had been murdered by that same ball, by the criminal or magical hand of an actor transformed by the words of Shakespeare into Marcus Brutus, Cæsar's murderer. In the mid-seventeenth century, vengeance had employed it for the assassination of Sweden's Gustavus Adolphus, in the midst of the public hecatomb of a battle.

In earlier times, the bullet had been other things, because Pythagorean metempsychosis is not reserved for humankind alone. It was the silken cord given to viziers in the East, the rifles and bayonets that cut down the defenders of the Alamo, the triangular blade that slit a queen's throat, the wood of the Cross and the dark nails that pierced the flesh of the Redeemer, the poison kept by the Carthaginian chief in an iron ring on his finger, the serene goblet that Socrates drank down one evening.

In the dawn of time it was the stone that Cain hurled at Abel, and in the future it shall be many things that we cannot even imagine today, but that will be able to put an end to men and their wondrous, fragile life.

Afterword

God grant that the essential monotony of this miscellany (which time has compiled, not I, and into which have been bundled long-ago pieces that I've not had the courage to revise, for I wrote them out of a different concept of literature) be less obvious than the geographical and historical diversity of its subjects. Of all the books I have sent to press, none, I think, is as personal as this motley, disorganized anthology, precisely because it abounds in reflections and interpolations. Few things have happened to me, though many things I have read. Or rather, few things have happened to me more worthy of remembering than the philosophy of Schopenhauer or England's verbal music.

A man sets out to draw the world. As the years go by, he peoples a space with images of provinces, kingdoms, mountains, bays, ships, islands, fishes, rooms, instruments, stars, horses, and individuals. A short time before he dies, he discovers that that patient labyrinth of lines traces the lineaments of his own face.

J.L.B.
Buenos Aires,
October 31, 1960

Afterword by Andrew Hurley

Jorge Luis Borges was an inveterate tinkerer, constantly fiddling with his stories and poems, rearranging their order, putting them in and taking them out of their original volumes, picking up a story or essay that he had published in a magazine years earlier and inserting it in a later collection, then having second thoughts and moving the piece to another volume altogether. And, of course, revising, rewriting, polishing; especially in the case of the poetry, changing or expunging lines, rethinking a single word or phrase, sometimes rewriting the entire poem. (The full story of Borges' revisions has yet to be written—perhaps, because so many manuscripts and publishers' galleys appear to be lost, it never will be.) So it should be no surprise that, like *Fictions*, the volume we know today as *The Aleph* passed through two major and two minor stages of growth (or diminution) as it evolved toward the form it has today. A first volume titled *The Aleph* and containing thirteen stories was published in 1949; that volume was expanded by four stories and published under the same title in 1952, and then one story, "The Interloper," was added in 1966 and then in a later edition taken out again.[1] Thus, today the volume consists of seventeen stories.

1. For the precise publishing information contained here, I wish most gratefully to acknowledge the important bibliographical work done by Nicolás Helft and published in *Jorge Luis Borges: Bibliografía completa* (Mexico City/Buenos Aires: Fondo de Cultura Económica, 1997).

Those of the book's first avatar began to appear as early as 1944, the same year that the second, expanded, and (relatively) definitive volume of *Fictions* was published. They appeared slowly, sporadically at first, in dribs and drabs, one in December of 1944 ("A Biography of Tadeo Isidoro Cruz"), one in September of 1945 ("The Aleph"), one in February of 1946 ("*Deutsches Requiem*"), and another in November of that same year ("The Dead Man"). These four stories all appeared in *Sur*, the prestigious literary magazine edited by Victoria Ocampo with which Borges had been associated since its inaugural number in 1931, but the next stories appeared in another venue.

This was a literary magazine published by an Argentine society resembling Paris's *Societé des Annales*; it was titled, unimaginatively if perhaps also not surprisingly, *Anales de Buenos Aires*. Borges' association with *Anales* began soon after the magazine was founded, when he was asked to be its editor; he took the reins beginning with the new publication's third number, in March of 1946. During that year, he contributed (both alone and jointly with his lifelong friend and collaborator Adolfo Bioy Casares) literally dozens of prose pieces to the magazine, all the while carrying out his editorial responsibilities. (One of the second-generation *Aleph* stories, a short piece called "The Story of the Two Kings and the Two Labyrinths," appeared in May of 1946 but was not to be collected in the volume until 1952.) By early 1947 Borges had begun to do fewer collaborative pieces, and a rush of new fictions destined for *The Aleph* began. In February of 1947 "The Immortal" was published (under the slightly different title "The Immortals"), and in quick succession from April to July four more stories: "The Theologians," "The House of Asterion," "Averroës' Search," and "The Zahir."

This flood of stories (relatively speaking, of course; Borges was never as prolific with his fictions as he was with book reviews and other sorts of more ephemeral literary essays) leads to an intriguing speculation about the nature of Borges' creative energies: is it possible that Borges worked much as scientists say a perpetual-motion machine might work, producing energy that can be used to do work or power other machines, and with enough left over to power itself? One is led to think of such a feedback mechanism for the creative energies because it seems that the more Borges worked at editing a magazine, at overseeing other people's stories, poems, book reviews, etc., at composing his own fictional or poetic contributions to those publications, at writing reviews and churning out other belletristic forms, at compiling anthologies and the like, and at writing introductions to other people's books and anthologies, the more stimulated he became creatively, and therefore the more of his own intriguing stories he produced. Consider this fact: during the time he was editing the weekly *Revista Multicolor* (1933–5) and producing scores of belletristic pieces for it (not to mention the essays that would show up years later in essay collections), he also produced the remarkable fictions of *A Universal History of Iniquity*. Or this fact: during the period when he and Adolfo Bioy Casares were collecting and publishing their *Anthology of Fantasy Literature* (December 1940) and he, Bioy, and Silvina Ocampo were compiling and publishing their *Anthology of Argentine Poetry* (late 1941), he was also producing the stories in *Fictions*, a book that Emir Rodríguez Monegal has called "perhaps the single most important book of prose fiction written in Spanish in this century." In that case, too, as he became more and more involved in the anthologies, the stories began with a hesitant (though literarily assured) dribbler, just a drop or two, and then swelled to a torrent, perhaps as the muse, or the perpetual-motion-machine energy, "kicked in." And now, again, the same phenomenon with *The Aleph*: new and very demanding editorial responsibilities; a new spate of fine stories.

By the end of 1947, Borges' association with *Anales de Buenos Aires* was coming to an end, and the review itself folded in early 1948. The other stories included in *The Aleph* would appear in *Sur* and *La Nación*, as his work had so often appeared in earlier years.

The next story to be published was in September of 1948; titled "Emma Zunz," it is one of Borges' most troubling stories, about a woman who premeditatedly stages her own rape in order to kill the "rapist" and thereby revenge her father's death. Then, in January, February, and May of 1949 came the last three stories of *The Aleph*'s first avatar: "The Other Death" (originally titled "The Redemption"), "The Writing of the God," and "Story of the Warrior and the Captive Maiden." With these pieces done, in June of 1949 Borges brought out *The Aleph*, a collection of stories "in the fantastic genre," as Borges described it. But his dismissive, almost trivializing description of the stories—of the *treatment* of the stories, their membership in a sub-literary genre—failed to note the seriousness of their themes: time and history, personal identity, human versus divine morality (or at least human ethics), "reality" versus "subjectivity," and the ground and role of litera-ture itself. Fortunately, readers were not taken in by Borges' modest assessment of the book.

The second edition of *The Aleph*, published in 1952, included four new stories: "The Wait," "Ibn-Hakam al-Bokhari, Murdered in His Labyrinth," "The Two Kings and the Two Labyrinths," and "The Man on the Threshold." These stories, with the exception of "The Two Kings" (mentioned above), appeared from August 1950 to April 1952, and in their somewhat fantastical cut resemble and round out the others.

Surely readers may be permitted to wonder why authors choose to give their short-story collections the title of one of the stories rather than another. The case of *The Aleph* is particularly intriguing, because except for the "fantastic genre" that Borges notes that almost all the stories belong to, at first glance they would seem to have little in common, thematically speaking. But that is first glance, and we know that Borges always richly repays a second, closer look. Thus, perhaps one might be excused for thinking out loud: the Aleph of the story's title is a most unsettling phenomenon, "a small iridescent sphere of almost unbearable brightness" tucked away under the stairs down in the basement of a house in Buenos Aires. The astounding thing about this tiny sphere, which is no more than two or three centimeters in diameter, is that it contains all of universal space, *with no diminution in size.* One of the characters in the story has discovered this marvelous Aleph and for years has gone down into the cellar to peer into it for material for a truly dreadful poem titled *The Earth*—a prosaic, uninspired poem (one is sorely tempted to call it idiotic) filled with tiny, meaningless details of a "geographical nature," as Borges might say. The narrator of the story, however, sees the Aleph in another way: he is dumbfounded by it, and would never think of merely *using* it. He describes it as "ineffable," as pure simultaneity, as unboundedness within its spherical bounds, and with great insight he notes that to describe similar experiences (for it is more *experience* than *thing*), mystics have used those famous images that we all know: a bird that is somehow all birds, a sphere whose center is everywhere and circumference nowhere, an angel with four faces. What is at the mysterious center of "The Aleph," then, is without doubt a mystical experience, the experience of Oneness, of Plenitude, of the All. That said, we might speculate that one of the motifs that Borges wanted to draw readers' attention to in this volume was the motif of knowledge, and specifically a knowledge that is at least potentially transfigurative. And indeed when we examine the stories, we find that many of them hinge on knowledge in one or another aspect: that knowledge which is, like God's, total, or the knowledge that the god would have us know ("The Theologians," "The Aleph," "The Writing of the God"); the transfiguration that occurs when one is struck by sudden knowledge ("The Writing of the God," "Emma Zunz," "The Dead Man"); the tragic or crippling lack of knowledge that one has searched for and yearned after but has not achieved or to which one remains blind ("The Immortal," "*Deutsches Requiem*," "Averroës' Search"). Other stories turn on an irony, the reverse of knowledge, ignorance: the reader "knows" more than the central character ("The House of Asterion," "*Deutsches Requiem*," "Averroës' Search"). Or on another sort of irony: what happens when knowledge (or perhaps false knowledge) "possesses" a person, instead of the other way around, producing an *idée fixe* ("Emma Zunz," "The Theologians," "The Zahir"). Several of the stories play out as puzzles or riddles or conundrums, in which the narrator or one of the characters acts almost like a detective, trying to solve a mystery; this is the case in "The Other Death," "The Man on the Threshold," and "Ibn-Hakam al-Bokhari." No one would pretend, of course, that this is the *only* motif at work in *The Aleph*, but certainly "blindness to knowledge" and "the blinding light of knowledge" figure large in virtually all the fictions. Nor would one presume to read Borges' mind in the matter of the title of the volume, but one asserts one's right to speculate. . . .

This collection (in both its first and second manifestations) garnered Borges great praise, as had the earlier *Fictions*. He was now being recognized as the "famous writer" that he would be for the rest of his long life, and Rodríguez Monegal has said that it is around this time that Borges fully became "Borges"— adopting that mask or persona not only recognized by interviewers and readers around the world but also employed from time to time by Borges the real, biographical creature as a character in his stories or a foil in his prose-poems. Perhaps, then, it is no wonder that another of the major themes of this collection of stories is, as I have noted, personal identity—sometimes a character questions it, sometimes loses it, sometimes fakes it, sometimes changes it (or appears to), sometimes sees it (or the author portrays it) through a "double" or a "mirror." Borges even borrows from literature and myth—Homer, the Minotaur, *Martín Fierro*—to explore the questions of who we "really" are, who we take ourselves to be, who others think we are or see us as, and how all those various "identities" interact.

In all of Borges' work, this question of personal identity is perhaps most famously addressed—and most hauntingly left hanging—in a prose-poem that Borges included in a 1960 collection of prose and poetry titled *The Maker*; the piece is titled "Borges and I," and it is one of Borges' most often quoted works. But however remarkable it may be, in terms of the motif of personal identity and personal existence it is in good company, for the prose pieces of *The Maker* continue to address, to grapple with, that intriguing issue; some of the pieces that take it up are "The Maker," "The Captive," "The Mountebank," "A Problem," "The Witness," "*Martín Fierro*," "*Everything and Nothing*," "*Inferno*, I, 32,*" and the haunting epitaph "In Memoriam, J.F.K."

These musings, cast as parables and questions about self and the world, about the poet and his created self and universe, about the avatars of self through time, are rounded out by an afterword whose last paragraph has often been cited as the perfect description of the phenomenon Borges/"Borges":

A man sets out to draw the world. As the years go by, he peoples a space with images of provinces, kingdoms, mountains, bays, ships, islands, fishes, rooms, instruments, stars, horses, and individuals. A short time before he dies, he discovers that that patient labyrinth of lines traces the lineaments of his own face.

These words movingly summarize that central motif of identity and self in these two collections of carefully compiled and unerringly crafted prose fictions, and surely are intriguing enough to stand as the last words of an introduction to, and invitation to explore, these fascinating labyrinths of knowledge.

Andrew Hurley
San Juan, Puerto Rico
January 2000

A Note on the Translation

(from *Collected Fictions*)

The first known English translation of a work of fiction by the Argentine Jorge Luis Borges appeared in the August 1948 issue of *Ellery Queen's Mystery Magazine*, but although seven or eight more translations appeared in "little magazines" and anthologies during the fifties, and although Borges clearly had his champions in the literary establishment, it was not until 1962, fourteen years after that first appearance, that a book-length collection of fiction appeared in English.

The two volumes of stories that appeared in that *annus mirabilis*—one from Grove Press, edited by Anthony Kerrigan, and the other from New Directions, edited by Donald A. Yates and James E. Irby—caused an impact that was immediate and overwhelming. John Updike, John Barth, Anthony Burgess, and countless other writers and critics have eloquently and emphatically attested to the unsettling yet liberating effect that Jorge Luis Borges' work had on their vision of the way literature was thenceforth to be done. Reading those stories, writers and critics encountered a disturbingly *other* writer (Borges seemed, sometimes, to come from a place even more distant than Argentina, another literary planet), transported into their ken by translations, who took the detective story and turned it into metaphysics, who took fantasy writing and made it, with its questioning and reinventing of everyday reality, central to the craft of fiction. Even as early as 1933, Pierre Drieu La Rochelle, editor of the influential *Nouvelle Revue Française*, returning to France after visiting Argentina, is famously reported to have said, "*Borges vaut le voyage*"; now, thirty years later, readers didn't have to make the long, hard (though deliciously exotic) journey into Spanish—Borges had been brought to them, and indeed he soon was being paraded through England and the United States like one of those New World indigenes taken back, captives, by Columbus or Sir Walter Raleigh, to captivate the Old World's imagination.

But while for many readers of these translations Borges was a new writer appearing as though out of nowhere, the truth was that by the time we were reading Borges for the first time in English, he had been writing for forty years or more, long enough to have become a self-conscious, self-possessed, and self-*critical* master of the craft.

The reader of the forewords to the fictions will note that Borges is forever commenting on the style of the stories or the entire volume, preparing the reader for what is to come stylistically as well as thematically. More than once he draws our attention to the "plain style" of the pieces, in contrast to his earlier "baroque." And he is right: Borges' prose style is characterized by a determined economy of resources in which every word is weighted, every word (every mark of punctuation) "tells." It is a quiet style, whose effects are achieved not with bombast or pomp, but rather with a single exploding word or phrase, dropped almost as though offhandedly into a quiet sentence: "He examined his wounds and saw, without astonishment, that they had healed." This laconic detail ("without astonishment"), coming at the very beginning of "The Circular Ruins," will probably only at the end of the story be recalled by the reader, who will, retrospectively and somewhat abashedly, see that it changes *everything* in the story; it is quintessential Borges.

Quietness, subtlety, a laconic terseness—these are the marks of Borges' style. It is a style that has often been called intellectual, and indeed it is dense with allusion—to literature, to philosophy, to religion or theology, to myth, to the culture and history of

Buenos Aires and Argentina and the Southern Cone of South America, to the other contexts in which his words may have appeared. But it is also a simple style: Borges' sentences are almost invariably classical in their symmetry, in their balance. Borges likes parallelism, chiasmus, subtle repetitions-with-variations; his only indulgence in "shocking" the reader (an effect he repudiated) may be the "Miltonian displacement of adjectives" to which he alludes in his foreword to *The Maker*.

Another clear mark of Borges' prose is its employment of certain words with, or for, their etymological value. Again, this is an adjectival device, and it is perhaps the technique that is most unsettling to the reader. One of the most famous opening lines in Spanish literature is this: *Nadie lo vio desembarcar en la unánime noche:* "No one saw him slip from the boat in the unanimous night." What an odd adjective, "unanimous." It is so odd, in fact, that other translations have not allowed it. But it is just as odd in Spanish, and it clearly responds to Borges' intention, explicitly expressed in such fictions as "The Immortal," to let the Latin root govern the Spanish (and, by extension, English) usage. There is, for instance, a "splendid" woman: Her red hair glows. If the translator strives for similarity of effect in the translation (as I have), then he or she cannot, I think, avoid using this technique— which is a technique that Borges' beloved Emerson and de Quincey and Sir Thomas Browne also used with great virtuosity.

Borges himself was a translator of some note, and in addition to the translations per se that he left to Spanish culture—a number of German lyrics, Faulkner, Woolf, Whitman, Melville, Carlyle, Swedenborg, and others—he left at least three essays on the act of translation itself. Two of these, I have found, are extraordinarily liberating to the translator. In "Versions of Homer" ("Las versiones homéricas," 1932), Borges makes it unmistakably clear that every translation is a "version"—not *the* translation of Homer (or any other author) but *a* translation, one in a never-ending series, at least an infinite *possible* series. The very idea of *the* (definitive) translation is misguided, Borges tells us; there are only drafts, approximations—*versions*, as he insists on calling them. He chides us: "The concept of 'definitive text' is appealed to only by religion, or by weariness." Borges makes the point even more emphatically in his later essay "The Translators of the 1001 Nights" ("Los traductores de las *1001 Noches*," 1935).

If my count is correct, at least seventeen translators have preceded me in translating one or more of the fictions of Jorge Luis Borges. In most translator's notes, the translator would feel obliged to justify his or her new translation of a classic, to tell the potential reader of this new *version* that the shortcomings and errors of those seventeen or so prior translations have been met and conquered, as though they were enemies. Borges has tried in his essays to teach us, however, that we should not translate "against" our predecessors; a new translation is always justified by the new voice given the old work, by the new life in a new land that the translation confers on it, by the "shock of the new" that both old and new readers will experience from this inevitably new (or renewed) work. What Borges teaches is that we should simply commend the translation to the reader, with the hope that the reader will find in it a literary experience that is rich and moving. I have listened to Borges' advice as I have listened to Borges' fictions, and I—like the translators who have preceded me—have rendered Borges in the style that I hear when I listen to him. I think that the reader of my version will hear something of the genius of his storytelling and his style. For those who wish to read Borges as Borges wrote Borges, there is always *le voyage à l'espagnol*.

The text that the Borges estate specified to be used for this new translation is the three-volume *Obras completas*, published by Emecé Editores in 1989.

In producing this translation, it has not been our intention to produce an annotated or scholarly edition of Borges, but rather a "reader's edition." Thus, bibliographical information (which is often confused or terribly complex even in the most reliable of cases) has not been included except in a couple of clear instances, nor have we taken variants into account in any way; the Borges Foundation is reported to be working on a fully annotated, bibliographically reasoned variorum, and scholars of course can go to the several bibliographies and many other references that now exist. I have, however, tried to provide the Anglophone reader with at least a modicum of the general knowledge of the history, literature, and culture of Argentina and the Southern Cone of South America that a Hispanophone reader of the fictions, growing up in that culture, would inevitably have. To that end, asterisks have been inserted into the text of the fictions, tied to corresponding notes at the back of the book. (The notes often cite sources where interested readers can find further information.)

One particularly thorny translation decision that had to be made involved *A Universal History of Iniquity*. This volume is purportedly a series of biographies of reprehensible evildoers, and as biography, the book might be expected to rely greatly upon "sources" of one sort or another—as indeed Borges' "Index of Sources" seems to imply. In his preface to the 1954 reprinting of the volume, however, Borges acknowledges the "fictive" nature of his stories: This is a case, he says, of "changing and distorting (sometimes without æsthetic justification) the stories of other men" to produce a work singularly his own. This sui generis use of sources, most of which were in English, presents the translator with something of a challenge: to translate Borges even while Borges is cribbing from, translating, and "changing and distorting" other writers' stories. The method I have chosen to employ is to go to the sources Borges names, to see the ground upon which those changes and distortions were wrought; where Borges is clearly translating phrases, sentences, or even larger pieces of text, I have used the English of the original source. Thus, the New York gangsters in "Monk Eastman" speak as Asbury quotes them, not as I might have translated Borges' Spanish into English had I been translating in the usual sense of the word; back-translating Borges' translation did not seem to make much sense. But even while returning to the sources, I have made no attempt, either in the text or in my notes, to "correct" Borges; he has changed names (or their spellings), dates, numbers, locations, etc., as his literary vision led him to, but the tracing of those "deviations" is a matter which the editors and I have decided should be left to critics and scholarly publications.

More often than one would imagine, Borges' characters are murderers, knife fighters, throat slitters, liars, evil or casually violent men and women—and of course many of them "live" in a time different from our own. They sometimes use language that is strong, and that today may well be offensive—words denoting membership in ethnic and racial groups, for example. In the Hispanic culture, however, some of these expressions can be, and often are, used as terms of endearment—*negro/negra* and *chino/china* come at once to mind. (I am not claiming that Argentina is free of bigotry; Borges chronicles that, too.) All this is to explain a decision as to my translation of certain terms—specifically *rusito* (literally "little Russian," but with the force of "Jew," "sheeny"), *pardo/parda* (literally "dark mulatto," "black-skinned"), and *gringo* (meaning Italian immigrants: "wops," etc.)—that Borges uses in his fictions. I have chosen to use the word "sheeny" for *rusito* and the word "wop" for *gringo* because in the stories in which these words appear, there is an intention to be offensive—a *character's* intention, not Borges'. I have also chosen to use the word "nigger" for *pardo/parda*. This decision is taken not without considerable soul-searching, but I feel there is historical justification for it. In the May 20, 1996, edition of *The New Yorker* magazine, p. 63, the respected historian and cultural critic Jonathan Raban noted the existence of a nineteenth-century "Nigger Bob's saloon," where, out on the Western frontier, husbands would await the arrival of the train bringing their wives from the East. Thus, when a character in one of Borges' stories says, "I knew I could count on you, old nigger," one can almost hear the slight tenderness, or respect, in the voice, even if, at the same time, one winces. In my view, it is not the translator's place to (as Borges put it) "soften or mitigate" these words. Therefore, I have translated the epithets with the words I believe would have been used in English—in the United States, say—at the time the stories take place.

The footnotes that appear throughout the text of the stories in the *Collected Fictions* are Borges' own, even when they say "Ed."

This translation commemorates the centenary of Borges' birth in 1899; I wish it also to mark the fiftieth anniversary of the first appearance of Borges in English, in 1948. It is to all translators, then, Borges included, that this translation is—unanimously—dedicated.

Andrew Hurley
San Juan, Puerto Rico
June 1998

Acknowledgments

(from *Collected Fictions*)

I am indebted to the University of Puerto Rico at Río Piedras for a sabbatical leave that enabled me to begin this project. My thanks to the administration, and to the College of Humanities and the Department of English, for their constant support of my work not only on this project but throughout my twenty-odd years at UPR.

The University of Texas at Austin, Department of Spanish and Portuguese, and its director, Madeline Sutherland-Maier, were most gracious in welcoming the stranger among them. The department sponsored me as a Visiting Scholar with access to all the libraries at UT during my three years in Austin, where most of this translation was produced. My sincerest gratitude is also owed those libraries and their staffs, especially the Perry-Castañeda, the Benson Latin American Collection, and the Humanities Research Center (HRC). Most of the staff, I must abashedly confess, were nameless to me, but one person, Cathy Henderson, has been especially important, as the manuscripts for this project have been incorporated into the Translator Archives in the HRC.

For many reasons this project has been more than usually complex. At Viking Penguin, my editors, Kathryn Court and Michael Millman, have been steadfast, stalwart, and (probably more often than they would have liked) inspired in seeing it through. One could not possibly have had more supportive colleagues, or co-conspirators who stuck by one with any greater solidarity.

Many, many people have given me advice, answered questions, and offered support of all kinds—they know who they are, and will forgive me, I know, for not mentioning them all personally; I have been asked to keep these acknowledgments brief. But two people, Carter Wheelock and Margaret Sayers Peden, have contributed in an especially important and intimate way, and my gratitude to them cannot go unexpressed here. Carter Wheelock read word by word through an "early-final" draft of the translation, comparing it against the Spanish for omissions, misperceptions and mistranslations, and errors of fact. This translation is the cleaner and more honest for his efforts. Margaret Sayers Peden (a.k.a. Petch), one of the finest translators from Spanish working in the world today, was engaged by the publisher to be an outside editor for this volume. Petch read through the late stages of the translation, comparing it with the Spanish, suggesting changes that ranged from punctuation to "readings." Translators want to translate, *love* to translate; for a translator at the height of her powers to read a translation in this painstaking way and yet, while suggesting changes and improvements, to respect the other translator's work, his approach, his thought processes and creativity—even to applaud the other translator's (very) occasional strokes of brilliance—is to engage in an act of selflessness that is almost superhuman. She made the usual somewhat tedious editing process a joy.

I would never invoke Carter Wheelock's and Petch Peden's readings of the manuscripts of this translation—or those of Michael Millman and the other readers at Viking Penguin—as giving it any authority or credentials or infallibility beyond its fair deserts, but I must say that those readings have given me a security in this translation that I almost surely would not have felt so strongly without them. I am deeply and humbly indebted.

First, last, always, and in number of words inversely proportional to my gratitude—I thank my wife, Isabel Garayta.

Andrew Hurley
San Juan, Puerto Rico
June 1998

Notes to the Fictions

(from *Collected Fictions*)

These notes are intended only to supply information that a Latin American (and especially Argentine or Uruguayan) reader would have and that would color or determine his or her reading of the stories. Generally, therefore, the notes cover only Argentine history and culture; I have presumed the reader to possess more or less the range of general or world history or culture that JLB makes constant reference to, or to have access to such reference books and other sources as would supply any need there. There is no intention here to produce an "annotated Borges," but rather only to illuminate certain passages that might remain obscure, or even be misunderstood, without that information.

For these notes, I am deeply indebted to *A Dictionary of Borges* by Evelyn Fishburn and Psiche Hughes (London: Duckworth, 1990). Other dictionaries, encyclopedias, reference books, biographies, and works of criticism have been consulted, but none has been as thorough and immediately useful as the *Dictionary of Borges*. In many places, and especially where I quote Fishburn and Hughes directly, I cite their contribution, but I have often paraphrased them without direct attribution; I would not want anyone to think, however, that I am unaware or unappreciative of the use I have made of them. Any errors are my own responsibility, of course, and should not be taken to reflect on them or their work in any way. Another book that has been invaluable is Emir Rodríguez Monegal's *Jorge Luis Borges: A Literary Biography* (New York: Paragon Press, [paper] 1988), now out of print. In the notes, I have cited this work as "Rodríguez Monegal, p. x."

The names of Arab and Persian figures that appear in the stories are taken, in the case of historical persons, from the English transliterations of Philip K. Hitti in his work *History of the Arabs from the Earliest Times to the Present* (New York: Macmillan, 1951). (JLB himself cites Hitti as an authority in this field.) In the case of fictional characters, the translator has used the system of transliteration implicit in Hitti's historical names in comparison with the same names in Spanish transliteration.—*Translator*.

The Aleph

The Dead Man

p. 20: Rio Grande do Sul: The southernmost state of Brazil, bordering both Argentina and Uruguay on the north. Later in this story, a certain wildness is attributed to this region; JLB often employed the implicit contrast between the more "civilized" city and province of Buenos Aires (and all of Argentina) and the less "developed" city of Montevideo and nation of Uruguay and its "wilderness of horse country," the "plains," "the interior," here represented by Rio Grande do Sul.

p. 20: Paso del Molino: "A lower-to-middle-class district outside Montevideo" (Fishburn and Hughes).

Story of the Warrior and the Captive Maiden

p. 38: The Auracan or Pampas tongue: The Pampas Indians were a nomadic people who inhabited the plains of the Southern Cone at the time of the Conquest; they were overrun by the Araucans, and the languages and cultures merged; today the two names are essentially synonymous (Fishburn and Hughes). English seems not to have taken the name Pampas for anything but the plains of Argentina.

p. 39: Pulpería: A country store or general store, though not the same sort of corner grocery-store-and-bar, the *esquina* or *almacén*, that Borges uses as a setting in the stories that take place in the city. The *pulpería* would have been precisely the sort of frontier general store that one sees in American westerns.

A Biography of Tadeo Isidoro Cruz (1829–1874)

p. 40: Montoneros: Montoneros were the men of guerrilla militias (generally gauchos) that fought in the civil wars following the wars of independence. They tended to rally under the banner of a leader rather than specifically under the banner of a cause; Fishburn and Hughes put it in the following way: "[T]heir allegiance to their leader was personal and direct, and they were largely indifferent to his political leanings."

p. 40: Lavalle: Juan Galo Lavalle (1797–1841) was an Argentine hero who fought on the side of the Unitarians, the centralizing Buenos Aires forces, against the Federalist *montoneros* of the outlying provinces and territories, whose most famous leader was Juan Manuel de Rosas, the fierce dictator who appears in several of JLB's stories. The mention here of Lavalle and López would indeed locate this story in 1829, a few months before Lavalle was defeated by the combined Rosas and López forces (Fishburn and Hughes). One would assume, then, that the man who fathered Tadeo Isidoro Cruz was fighting with Rosas' forces themselves.

p. 40: Suárez' cavalry: Probably Manuel Isidoro Suárez (1759–1843), JLB's mother's maternal grandfather, who fought on the side of the Unitarians in the period leading up to 1829 (Fishburn and Hughes). Borges may have picked up the protagonist's name, as well, in part from his forebear.

p. 41: Thirty Christian men . . . Sgt. Maj. Eusebio Laprida . . . two hundred Indians: Eusebio Laprida (1829–1898) led eighty, not thirty, men against a regular army unit of two hundred soldiers, not Indians, in a combat at the Cardoso Marshes on January 25, not 23, 1856 (data, Fishburn and Hughes). The defeat of the Indians took place during a raid in 1879. JLB here may be conflating the famous Thirty-three led by Lavalleja against Montevideo (see note to "Avelino Arredondo" in *The Book of Sand*), Laprida's equally heroic exploit against a larger "official" army unit, and Laprida's exploit against the Indians two decades later.

p. 42: Manuel Mesa executed in the Plaza de la Victoria: Manuel Mesa (1788–1829) fought on the side of Rosas and the Federalists. In 1829 he organized a force of *montoneros* and friendly Indians and battled Lavalle, losing that engagement. In his retreat, he was met by Manuel Isidoro Suárez and captured. Suárez sent him to Buenos Aires, where he was executed in the Plaza Victoria.

p. 43: The deserter Martín Fierro: As JLB tells the reader in the Afterword to this volume, this story has been a retelling, from the "unexpected" point of view of a secondary character, of the famous gaucho epic poem *Martín Fierro*, by José Hernández. Since this work is a classic (or *the* classic) of nineteenth-century Argentine literature, every reader in the Southern Cone would recognize "what was coming": Martín Fierro, the put-upon gaucho hero, stands his ground against the authorities, and his friend abandons his uniform to stand and fight with him. This changing sides is a recurrent motif in Borges; see "Story of the Warrior and the Captive Maiden" in this volume, for instance. It seems to have been more interesting to JLB that one might change sides than that one would exhibit the usual traits of heroism. Borges is also fond of rewriting classics: See "The House of Asterion," also in this volume, and note that the narrator in "The Zahir" retells to himself, more or less as the outline of a story he is writing, the story of the gold of the Nibelungen. One could expand the list to great length.

Emma Zunz

p. 44: Bagé: A city in southern Rio Grande do Sul province, in Brazil.

p. 45: Gualeguay: "A rural town and department in the province of Entre Ríos" (Fishburn and Hughes).

p. 45: Lanús: "A town and middle-class district in Greater Buenos Aires, southwest of the city" (Fishburn and Hughes).

p. 46: Almagro: A lower-middle-class neighborhood near the center of Buenos Aires.

p. 46: Calle Liniers: As the story says, a street in the Almagro neighborhood.

p. 46: Paseo de Julio: Now the Avenida Alem. This street runs parallel with the waterfront; at the time of this story it was lined with tenement houses and houses of ill repute.

p. 47: A westbound Lacroze: The Lacroze Tramway Line served the northwestern area of Buenos Aires at the time; today the city has an extensive subway system.

p. 48: Warnes: A street in central Buenos Aires near the commercial district of Villa Crespo, where the mill is apparently located.

The Other Death

p. 54: Gualeguaychú: "A town on the river of the same name in the province of Entre Ríos, opposite the town of Fray Bentos, with which there is considerable interchange" (Fishburn and Hughes).

p. 54: Masoller: Masoller, in northern Uruguay, was the site of a decisive battle on September 1, 1904, between the rebel forces of Aparicio Saravia (see below) and the National Army; Saravia was defeated and mortally wounded (Fishburn and Hughes).

p. 54: The banners of Aparicio Saravia: Aparicio Saravia (1856–1904) was a Uruguayan landowner and caudillo who led the successful Blanco (White party) revolt against the dictatorship of Idiarte Borda (the Colorados, or Red party). Even in victory, however, Saravia had to continue to fight against the central government, since Borda's successor, Batlle, refused to allow Saravia's party to form part of the new government. It is the years of this latter revolt that are the time of "The Other Death." See also, for a longer explanation of the political situation of the time, the story "Avelino Arredondo" in *The Book of Sand.*

p. 54: Río Negro or Paysandú: Río Negro is the name of a department in western Uruguay on the river of the same name, just opposite the Argentine province of Entre Ríos. Paysandú is a department in Uruguay bordering Río Negro. Once again JLB is signaling the relative "wildness" of Uruguay in comparison with Argentina, which was not touched by these civil wars at the time.

p. 54: Gualeguay: See note to p. 44 above. Note the distinction between "Gualeguay" and "Gualeguaychú" (see note to p. 54 above).

p. 54: Ñancay: "A tributary of the Uruguay River that flows through the rich agricultural lands of southern Entre Ríos province" (Fishburn and Hughes).

p. 55: Men whose throats were slashed through to the spine: This is another instance in which JLB documents the (to us today) barbaric custom by the armies of the South American wars of independence (and other, lesser combats as well) of slitting defeated troops' throats. In other places, he notes offhandedly that "no prisoners were taken," which does not mean that all the defeated troops were allowed to return to their bivouacs. In this case, a rare case, Borges actually "editorializes" a bit: "a civil war that struck me as more some outlaw's dream than the collision of two armies."

p. 55: Illescas, Tupambaé, Masoller: All these are the sites of battles in northern and central Uruguay fought in 1904 between Saravia's forces and the National Army of Uruguay.

p. 56: White ribbon: Because the troops were often irregulars, or recruited from the gauchos or farmhands of the Argentine, and therefore lacking standardized uniforms, the only way to tell friend from enemy was by these ribbons, white in the case of the Blancos, red in the case of the Colorados. Here the white ribbon worn by the character marks him as a follower of Saravia, the leader of the Whites. (See notes *passim* about the significance of these parties.)

p. 56: Zumacos: The name by which regulars in the Uruguayan National Army were known.

p. 56: Artiguismo: That is, in accord with the life and views of José Gervasio Artigas (1764–1850), a Uruguayan hero who fought against both the Spaniards and the nascent Argentines to forge a separate nation out of what had just been the Banda Oriental, or east bank of the Plate. The argument was that Uruguay had its own "spirit," its own "sense of place," which the effete Argentines of Buenos Aires, who only romanticized the gaucho but had none of their own, could never truly understand or live.

p. 57: Red infantry: The Reds, or Colorados, were the forces of the official national government of Uruguay, in contradistinction to the Blancos, or Whites, of Saravia's forces; the Reds therefore had generally better weapons and equipment, and better-trained military officers on the whole, than the irregular and largely gaucho Whites.

p. 57: ¿Viva Urquiza!: Justo José Urquiza (1801–1870) was president of the Argentinian Confederation between 1854 and 1860. Prior to that, he had fought with the Federalists under Rosas (the provincial forces) against the Unitarians (the Buenos Aires-based centralizing forces), but in 1845 he broke with Rosas (whom JLB always excoriates as a vicious dictator) and eventually saw Buenos Aires province and the other provinces of the Argentinian Confederation brought together into the modern nation of Argentina, though under the presidency of Bartolomé Mitre.

p. 57: Cagancha or India Muerta: The perplexity here derives from the fact that while the battle at Masoller, in which Damián took part, occurred in 1904, the cry ¿*Viva Urquiza!* would have been heard at the Battle of Cagancha (1839) or India Muerta (1845), where Urquiza's rebel Federalist forces fought the Unitarians. At Cagancha, Urquiza was defeated by the Unitarians; at India Muerta he defeated them. This story may also, thus, have certain subterranean connections with "The

Theologians," in its examination of the possibilities of repeating or circular, or at least nondiscrete, time.

p. 59: He "marked" no one: He left his mark on no man in a knife fight; in a fight, when the slight might, even by the standards of the day, be deemed too inconsequential to kill a man for, or if the other man refused to fight, the winner would leave his mark, a scar, that would settle the score.

Averroës' Search

p. 74: "The seven sleepers of Ephesus": This is a very peculiar story to put in the minds of these Islamic luminaries, for the story of the seven sleepers of Ephesus is a Christian story, told by Gregory of Tours. Clearly the breadth of culture of these gentlemen is great, but it is difficult (at least for this translator) to see the relationship of this particular tale (unlike the other "stories," such as the children playing or "representing" life and the "if it had been a snake it would have bitten him" story told by abu-al-Hasan) to Averroës' quest.

The Zahir

p. 80: Calle Aráoz: Fishburn and Hughes tell us that in the 1930s, Calle Aráoz was "a street of small houses inhabited by the impoverished middle class"; it is near the penitentiary Las Heras.

p. 81: On the corner of Chile and Tacuarí: A corner in the Barrio Sur, or southern part of Buenos Aires, as the story says; it is some ten blocks from the Plaza Constitución and its great station.

p. 81: Truco: A card game indigenous, apparently, to Argentina and played very often in these establishments. Borges was fascinated by this game and devoted an essay and two or three poems to it, along with references, such as this one, scattered throughout his œuvre. The phrase "to my misfortune" indicates the inexorability of the attraction that the game held for him; the narrator could apparently simply not avoid going into the bar. Truco's nature, for JLB, is that combination of fate and chance that seems to rule over human life as well as over games: an infinitude of possibilities within a limited number of cards, the limitations of the rules. See "Truco" in *Borges: A Reader*.

p. 82: La Concepción: A large church in the Barrio Sur, near the Plaza Constitución.

p. 82: The chamfered curb in darkness: Here JLB's reference is to an *ochava*—that is, a "corner with the corner cut off" to form a three-sided, almost round curb, and a somewhat wider eight-sided rather than four-sided intersection, as the four corners of the intersection would all be chamfered in that way. This reference adds to the "old-fashioned" atmosphere of the story, because chamfered corners were common on streets traveled by large horse-drawn wagons, which would need extra space to turn the corners so that their wheels would not ride up onto the sidewalks.

p. 83: I went neither to the Basílica del Pilar that morning nor to the cemetery: That is, the narrator did not go to Teodelina's funeral. The Basílica del Pilar is one of the most impressive churches in central Buenos Aires, near the Recoleta cemetery where Teodelina Vilar would surely have been buried.

p. 87: "She's been put into Bosch": Bosch was "a well-known private clinic frequented by the *porteño* elite" (Fishburn and Hughes).

The Writing of the God

p. 93: I saw the origins told by the Book of the People. I saw . . . the dogs that tore at their faces: Here the priest is remembering the story of the creation of the world told in the Popul Vuh, the Mayan sacred text. The standard modern translation is by Dennis Tedlock: *Popul Vuh: The Mayan Book of the Dawn of Life* (New York: Simon & Schuster Touchstone, 1985).

The Wait

p. 109: Plaza del Once: Pronounced *óhn-say*, not *wunce.* This is actually "Plaza Once," but the homonymy of the English and Spanish words makes it advisable, I think, to modify the name slightly in order to alert the English reader to the Spanish ("eleven"), rather than the English ("onetime" or "past"), sense of the word. Plaza Once is one of Buenos Aires' oldest squares, "associated in Borges's memory with horse-drawn carts" (Fishburn and Hughes), though later simply a modern square.

The Aleph

p. 119: Quilmes: A district in southern Buenos Aires; "at one time favoured for weekend villas, particularly by the British, Quilmes has since become unfashionable, a heavily industrialised area, known mainly for Quilmes Beer, the largest brewing company in the world" (Fishburn and Hughes). Thus JLB is evoking a world of privilege and luxe.

p. 121: Juan Crisóstomo Lafinur Library: This library is named after JLB's great-uncle (1797–1824), who occupied the chair of philosophy at the Colegio de la Unión del Sud until, under attack for teaching materialism, he was forced into exile.

p. 124: "The most elevated heights of Flores": Here Daneri's absurdity reaches "new heights," for though the neighborhood of Flores had been very much in vogue among the affluent of Buenos Aires society during the nineteenth century, it was only about a hundred feet above sea level. Moreover, it had lost much of its exclusiveness, and therefore glamour, by the time of this story, since in the yellow fever epidemic of 1871 people fled "central" Buenos Aires for the "outlying" neighborhood.

p. 130: Chacarita: One of the two enormous cemeteries in Buenos Aires; the other is Recoleta. A modern guidebook* has this to say about the cemeteries of Buenos Aires:

Life and Death in Recoleta & Chacarita

Death is an equalizer, except in Buenos Aires. When the arteries harden after decades of dining at Au Bec Fin and finishing up with coffee and dessert at La Biela or Café de la Paix, the wealthy and powerful of Buenos Aires move ceremoniously across the street to Recoleta Cemetery, joining their forefathers in a place they have visited religiously all their lives. . . . According to Argentine novelist Tomás Eloy Martínez, Argentines are "cadaver cultists" who honor their most revered national figures not on the date of their birth but of their death. . . . Nowhere is this obsession with mortality and corruption more evident than in Recoleta, where generations of the elite repose in the grandeur of ostentatious mausoleums. It is a common saying and only a slight exaggeration that "it is cheaper to live extravagantly all your life than to be buried in Recoleta." Traditionally, money is not enough: you must have a surname like Anchorena, Alvear, Aramburu, Avellaneda, Mitre, Martínez de Hoz, or Sarmiento. . . .

Although more democratic in conception, Chacarita has many tombs which match the finest in Recoleta. One of the most visited belongs to Carlos Gardel, the famous tango singer. (*Argentina, Uruguay & Paraguay, *Wayne Bernhardson and María Massolo, Hawthorne, Vic, Australia; Berkeley, CA, USA; and London, UK: Lonely Planet Publications [Travel Survival Kit], 1992)*

p. 132: Compendia of Dr. Acevedo Díaz: Eduardo Acevedo Díaz (1882–1959) won the Premio Nacional for his novel *Cancha Larga*; JLB's entry that year, *The Garden of Forking Paths*, won second prize.

p. 133: Pedro Henríquez Ureña: Henríquez Ureña (1884–1946), originally from the Dominican Republic, lived for years in Buenos Aires and was an early contributor to *Sur*, the magazine that Victoria Ocampo founded and that JLB assiduously worked on. It was through Henríquez Ureña, who had lived for a time in Mexico City, that JLB met another close friend, the Mexican humanist Alfonso Reyes. Henríquez Ureña and JLB collaborated on the *Antología de la literatura argentina* (1937).

The Maker

Foreword

p. 139: Leopoldo Lugones: Lugones (1874–1938) was probably Argentina's leading poet in the second to fourth decades of this century; he was influenced by Spanish *modernismo* and by the French Symbolists. To a degree he represented to the young Turks of Argentine poetry the *ancien régime*; therefore he was often attacked, and often tastelessly so. Early on, JLB joined in these gibes at Lugones, though clearly Borges also recognized Lugones' skills and talents as a poet. Rodríguez Monegal speculates that JLB had mixed feelings about Lugones, especially in his person, but suggests that respect for Lugones as a poet no doubt prevailed, especially as JLB matured. Monegal quotes Borges (quoted by Fernández Moreno) as follows: Lugones was "a solitary and dogmatic man, a man who did not open up easily. . . .Conversation was difficult with him because he [would] bring everything to a close with a phrase which was literally a period. . . .Then you had to begin again, to find another subject. . . .And that subject was also dissolved with a period. . . .His kind of conversation was brilliant but tiresome. And many times his assertions had nothing to do with what he really believed; he just had to say something extraordinary. . . .What he wanted was to control the conversation. Everything he said was final. And . . . we had a great respect for him." (Fernández Moreno [1967], pp. 10–11, in Rodríguez Monegal, p. 197; ellipses in Rodríguez Monegal.) Another problem with Lugones was his partiality to military governments, his proto- and then unfeigned fascism; obviously this did not endear him to many, more liberal, thinkers. In this introduction JLB seems to recognize that while he and his friends were experimenting with a "new" poetics in the first decades of the century, Lugones kept on his amiable way, and to admit that later he, JLB, had put aside some of the more shocking and radical of his notions of poetry in favor of a cleaner, less "poetic" poetry, which Lugones would probably have recognized as much closer to his own. So the "son" comes to see that he has come to resemble the resented "father" (no Freudian implications intended; genetics only; no political implications intended, either; Borges hated military governments and hated fascism and Nazism).

p. 140: The Maker: The Spanish title of this "heterogeneous" volume of prose and poetry (only the prose is included in this volume) is *El hacedor,* and *hacedor* is a troublesome word for a translator into English. JLB seems to be thinking of the Greek word *poeta,* which means "maker," since a "true and literal" translation of *poeta* into Spanish would indeed be *hacedor.* Yet *hacedor* is in this translator's view, and in the view of all those native speakers he has consulted, a most uncommon word. It is not used in Spanish for "poet" but instead makes one think of someone who makes things with his hands, a kind of artisan, perhaps, or perhaps even a tinkerer. The English word *maker* is perhaps strange too, yet it exists; however, it is used in English (in such phrases as "he went to meet his Maker" and the brand name Maker's Mark) in a way that dissuades one from seizing upon it immediately as the "perfect" translation for *hacedor.* (The Spanish word *hacedor* would never be used for "God," for instance.) Eliot Weinberger has suggested to me, quite rightly, perhaps, that JLB had in mind the Scots word *makir,* which means "poet." But there are other cases: Eliot's dedication of *The Waste Land* to Ezra Pound, taken from Dante—*il miglior fabbro,* where *fabbro* has exactly the same range as *hacedor.* Several considerations seem to militate in favor of the translation "artificer": first, the sense of someone's making something with his hands, or perhaps "sculptor," for one of JLB's favorite metaphors for poetry was at one time sculpture; second, the fact that the second "volume" in the volume *Fictions* is clearly titled *Artifices*; third, the overlap between art and craft or artisanry that is implied in the word, as in the first story in this volume. But a translational decision of this kind is never easy and perhaps never "done"; one wishes one could call the volume *Il fabbro*, or *Poeta*, or leave it *El hacedor*. The previous English translation of this volume in fact opted for *Dreamtigers*. Yet sometimes a translator is spared this anguish (if he or she finds the key to the puzzle in time to forestall it); in this case there is an easy solution. I quote from Emir Rodríguez Monegal's *Jorge Luis Borges: A Literary Biography*, p. 438: "Borges was sixty when the ninth volume of his complete works came out. . . .For the new book he had thought up the title in English: *The Maker*, and had translated it into Spanish as *El hacedor*; but when the book came out in the United States the American translator preferred to avoid the theological implications and used instead the title of one of the pieces: *Dreamtigers*." And so a translation problem becomes a problem *created* in the first place by a translation! (Thanks to Eliot Weinberger for coming across this reference *in time* and bringing it to my attention.)

Dreamtigers

p. 143: Title: The title of this story appears in italics because JLB used the English nonce word in the Spanish original.

p. 143: That spotted "tiger": While there are many indigenous words for the predatory cats of South America—puma, jaguar, etc.—that have been adopted into Spanish, Peninsular Spanish called these cats tigers. (One should recall that Columbus simply had no words for the myriad new things in this New World, so if an indigenous word did not "catch on" immediately, one was left with a European word for the thing: hence "Indians"!) Here, then, JLB is comparing the so-called tiger of the Southern Cone with its Asian counterpart, always a more intriguing animal for him. Cf., for instance, "Blue Tigers" in the volume titled *Shakespeare's Memory*.

Toenails

p. 145: Recoleta: The "necropolis" near the center of Buenos Aires, where the elite of Porteño society buries its dead. See also note to "The Aleph."

Covered Mirrors

p. 146: Federalists/Unitarians: The Federalists were those nine-teenth-century conservatives who favored a federal (i.e., decentralized) plan of government for Argentina, with the provinces having great autonomy and an equal say in the government; the Federalists were also "Argentine," as opposed to the internationalist, Europe-looking Unitarians, and their leaders tended to be populist caudillos, their fighters in the civil wars to be gauchos. The Unitarians, on the other hand, were a Buenos Aires-based party that was in favor of a centralizing, liberal government; they tended to be "free-thinkers," rather than Catholics *per se*, intellectuals, internationalists, and Europophile in outlook. Unitarians deplored the barbarity of the gaucho ethos, and especially sentimentalizing that way of life; they were urban to a fault. This old "discord between their lineages," as Borges puts it in this story, is the discord of Argentina, never truly overcome in the Argentina that JLB lived in.

p. 147: Balvanera: One can assume that at the time "Borges" had this experience, Balvanera was a neighborhood of "genteel poverty" much as one might envision it from the description of "Julia," but in the story "The Dead Man," Balvanera is the neighborhood that the "sad sort of hoodlum" Benjamín Otálora comes from, and it is described as a district on the outskirts of the Buenos Aires of 1891 (which does not, emphatically, mean that it would be on the outskirts of the Buenos Aires of 1927, the time of the beginning of "Covered Mirrors"), a neighborhood of "cart drivers and leather braiders." Thus Balvanera is associated not so much with gauchos and cattle (though the Federalist connection hints at such a connotation) as with the stockyards and their industries, the *secondary* (and romantically inferior) spin-offs of the pampas life. Balvanera here, like Julia's family itself, is the decayed shadow of itself and the life it once represented.

p. 147: Blank wall of the railway yard ... Parque Centenario: The railway ran (and runs) through Balvanera from the Plaza del Once station westward, out toward the outskirts of Buenos Aires. Sarmiento runs westward, too, but slightly north of the railway line, and running slightly northwest. It meets the Parque Centenario about a mile and a half from the station.

The Mountebank

p. 151: Chaco River: In the Litoral region of northern Argentina, an area known for cattle raising and forestry.

Delia Elena San Marco

p. 153: Plaza del Once (pronounced *óhn-say*, not *wunce*). This is actually usually given as Plaza Once, but the homonymy of the English and Spanish words makes it advisable, I think, to modify the name slightly so as to alert the English reader to the Spanish ("eleven"), rather than English ("onetime" or "past"), sense of the word. JLB himself uses "Plaza del Once" from time to time, as in the *Obras completas*, vol. II, p. 428, in the story "La señora mayor," in *Informe de Brodie* ("The Elderly Lady," in *Brodie's Report*, p. 375). Plaza Once is one of Buenos Aires' oldest squares, "associated in Borges's memory with horse-drawn carts" (Fishburn and Hughes), though later simply a modern square, and now the site of Buenos Aires' main train station for westbound railways.

A Dialog Between Dead Men

p. 155: Quiroga: Like many of the pieces in this volume ("The Captive," "*Martín Fierro*," "*Everything and Nothing*"), "A Dialog Between Dead Men" sets up a "dialog" with others of Borges' writings, especially a famous poem called "General Quiroga Rides to His Death in a Carriage" ("El general Quiroga va en coche al muere [*sic*, for "*a su muerte, a la muerte*," etc.]"). There the reader will find the scene that is not described but only alluded to here, the murder of General Quiroga by a sword-wielding gang of horsemen under the leadership of the Reinafé brothers. Some biographical information is essential here: Juan Facundo Quiroga (1793–1835) was a Federalist caudillo (which means that he was on the side of Rosas [see below]), and was, like Rosas, a leader feared by all and hated by his opponents; he was known for his violence, cruelty, and ruthlessness and made sure that his name was feared by slitting the throats of the prisoners that his forces captured and of the wounded in the battles that he fought. So great was his charisma, and so ruthless his personality, that his supposed ally in the fight against the Unitarians, Juan Manuel de Rosas, began to resent (and perhaps mistrust) him. As Quiroga was leaving a meeting with Rosas in 1835, he was ambushed by the Reinafé gang, and he and his companions were brutally murdered, their bodies hacked to pieces; it was widely believed (though stubbornly denied by Rosas) that Rosas had ordered the assassination.

p. 155: Rosas: Juan Manuel de Rosas (1793–1877) was the dictator of Argentina for eighteen years, from 1835 to 1852. His dictatorship was marked by terror and persecution, and he is for JLB one of the most hated figures in Argentine history; JLB's forebears, Unitarians, suffered the outrages of Rosas and his followers. Early in his career Rosas was a Federalist (later the distinction became meaningless, as Rosas did more than anyone to unify Argentina, though most say he did so for all the wrong reasons), a caudillo whose followers were gangs of gauchos and his own private vigilante force, the so-called *mazorca* (see the story "Pedro Salvadores" in *In Praise of Darkness*). He methodically persecuted, tortured, and killed off his opponents both outside *and inside* his party, until he at last reigned supreme over the entire country. See the poem "Rosas" in JLB's early volume of poetry *Fervor de Buenos Aires*.

p. 156: "Chacabuco and Junín and Palma Redondo and Caseros": Battles in the wars of independence of the countries of the Southern Cone.

The Yellow Rose

p. 160: Porpora de' giardin, pompa de' prato, / Gemma di primavera, occhio d'aprile ... : These lines are from a poem, *L'Adone*, written by Marino (1569–1625) himself (III:158, II. 1–2).

Martín Fierro

p. 163: Ituzaingó or Ayacucho: Battles (1827 and 1824 respectively) in the wars of independence against Spain.

p. 163: Peaches ... a young boy ... the heads of Unitarians, their beards bloody: This terrible image captures the cruelty and horror of the civil war that racked Argentina in the early nineteenth century, and the brutality with which the Federalists, when they were in power under Rosas, persecuted and terrorized the Unitarians. In other stories I have noted that slitting throats was the preferred method of dispatching captured opponents and the wounded of battles; here the opponents are decapitated. Making this all the more horrific is the fact that it was JLB's maternal grandfather, Isidoro Acevedo, who as a child witnessed this scene. In *JLB: Selected Poems 1923–1967* (Harmondsworth: Penguin, 1985), p. 316, the editor quotes Borges (without further citation): "One day, at the age of nine or ten, he [Isidoro Acevedo] walked by the Plata Market. It was in the time of Rosas. Two gaucho teamsters were hawking peaches. He lifted the canvas covering the fruit, and there were the decapitated heads of Unitarians, with blood-stained beards and wide-open eyes. He ran home, climbed up into the grapevine growing in the back patio, and it was only later that night that he could bring himself to tell what he had seen in the morning. In time, he was to see many things during the civil wars, but none ever left so deep an impression on him."

p. 163: A man who knew all the words . . . metaphors of metal . . . the shapes of its moon: This is probably Leopoldo Lugones. See the note, above, to the foreword to *The Maker,* p. 209.

Paradiso, *XXXI, 108*

p. 167: "My Lord Jesus Christ, . . . is this, indeed, Thy likeness in such fashion wrought?": Borges is translating Dante, *Paradiso,* XXXI: 108–109; in English, the lines read as given. Quoted from *The Portable Dante,* ed. Paolo Milano, *Paradiso,* trans. Laurence Binyon (1869–1943) (New York: Penguin, 1975 [orig. copyright, 1947]), p. 532.

Everything and Nothing

p. 171: Title: In italics here because the story was titled originally in this way by JLB, in English.

Ragnarök

p. 174: Pedro Henríquez Ureña: Henríquez Ureña (1884–1946), originally from the Dominican Republic, lived for years in Buenos Aires and was an early contributor to *Sur,* the magazine that Victoria Ocampo founded and that JLB assiduously worked on. It was through Henríquez Ureña, who had lived for a time in Mexico City, that JLB met another friend, the Mexican humanist Alfonso Reyes. Henríquez Ureña and JLB collaborated on the *Antología de la literatura argentina* (1937), and they were very close friends.

In Memoriam, J.F.K.

p. 182: Avelino Arredondo: The assassin, as the story says, of the president of Uruguay, Juan Idiarte Borda (1844–1897). See the story "Avelino Arredondo" in the volume *The Book of Sand.*